KEN JOHNSON

based on an original screenplay by
Jeff Lieberman

Encyclopocalypse Publications
www.encyclopocalypse.com

FOREWORD
BY JEFF LIEBERMAN

It was the winter of 1976 when I jotted down this hypothetical question on a yellow legal pad. "What if LSD chromosome damage was real?!"

Millions among my generation had experimented with LSD during the late 60's into the 70's. Deep down they all must harbor a fear there could be some validity to the our government's claims about the detrimental long-term effects of this mysterious drug. Why not tap into that fear the way Hollywood tapped into our generation's fear of the atomic bomb back in the fifties? What if there was a particular strain of LSD that altered our chromosomes the way those government 'experts' claimed radiation did?

Since the accepted aftereffects of LSD were flashbacks occurring weeks or even months after taking the drug, what if, instead of flashbacks, a certain strain of acid triggered a genetic mutation that turned a person into a human time bomb of unfettered violence? And of course, this drug would kick in just when the baby boomers who took it back, say, ten years ago in 1967, are now becoming the establishment, even having children of their own like I did, buying houses and settling into family life like their parents did.

First thing I needed was a title, which I instinctively knew should be the name of the LSD that causes this to happen. I jotted down all the names of acid brands, 'Blue Cheer,' 'Owsley Purple,' 'Orange Sunshine.' Then I mixed the words around to make up a fictional strain, that would also serve as a cool sounding movie title. I finally arrived at 'Blue Sunshine', then flipped to a new page and wrote that title again at the top, then started writing the screenplay in longhand.

The plot centered around a specific batch of LSD that was sold around the Syracuse University campus in upstate New York back in 1967. The movie took place ten years later when those who did the drug back then were now upstanding citizens including among them a doctor, a police officer and a congressional candidate. Though totally unaware, each of the Blue Sunshine recipients were a walking time bomb ready to explode into psychopathic killers.

My father suddenly suffered a fatal heart attack at the age of 55 and I was devastated and literally couldn't function. I expressed my grief with anger, lashing out at everyone around me.

Blue Sunshine was budgeted at three million dollars which included shooting on the streets and subways of New York, with flash backs to the 60's college campus scene.

Three million was a very big budget for a genre movie in those days and I couldn't wait for the producers to find that much money, I needed to immerse myself in work right then and there or I'd go insane. So, my Producers, Edgar Lansbury and Joe Beruh who also produced *Squirm,* agreed to finance it themselves, but for a fraction of the standing budget. A half million dollars. This necessitated not only cutting out all the 60's flashbacks to the Syracuse campus I had planned, but also meant we needed to shoot the movie in Los Angeles because the original setting described in my script was in and around New York city and its subway scenes alone were way beyond our financial reach.

Three months later we were in pre- production in Los Angeles, with George Manasse, my line producer on *Squirm*, serving as producer.

The standard procedure for these 'Soon to be a major motion picture' promotional paperbacks was for these writers-for-hire to be given an advance peek at the finished movie, then transcribe it to novelization form.

But for some strange reason which is still a mystery to me, writer Ken Johnson worked from my original New York set draft screenplay of *Blue Sunshine*, not the movie, which makes this re-issue completely unique. If you've seen the movie, the contrast and impact the change of locations had on the finished product will be apparent from the first page. If this is your introduction to *Blue Sunshine*, you'll experience firsthand the gritty, much deeper story I wanted to tell.

Jeff Lieberman
January 2024

BLUE SUNSHINE

CHAPTER 1

FEBRUARY CAME in like a wispy specter with a scythe, hard and finely-honed, slicing through the city while several million central heating units hummed back their defiance of the bitter cold. Whoever said April was the cruelest month probably went south in February.

The lights of the Metropolitan Hospital, in their neatly serried rows, shone golden in the Manhattan night like a network of illuminated honeycombs. Which was apt because, inside, the place was exactly like a beehive, twenty-four hours a day, seven days a week. Inside, the rattle of cutlery and stainless-steel tureens and plates and cups and saucers and beakers echoed along the basement corridors from the steam bath depths of the kitchens and up the elevator shafts and stairwells so that you could still hear the clatter, faintly, up on the fifth floor. The porters and catering staff crashed open the flapping swing doors with their wheeled trolleys, bringing in the debris from the evening meal.

In other parts, white-jacketed orderlies clanked to and fro in the labyrinthine passageways, hauling other trolley loads of soiled linen, lab equipment, trays of bottled drugs and medicines, towels, catheters and bedpans, like they were stewards on some giant luxury liner. Nurses in their uniforms, starched and pressed, scurried everywhere, up and down staircases and elevators, in and out of wards and offices, residences and operating theaters, always in a hurry, pristine white, ready for anything, anytime, because this was the way the ship is run. The patients rolled in and out, day and night, like a choppy tide, to the wail of ambulance sirens. A wave of them would wash in, right over the heads of the staff, and just as they were catching their breath, in rolled another one, and another and another and on like that forever.

Then there were the doctors, the key men and women. The whole thing was planned and timed and designed and angled around them. They were the ones, after all, who more or less decided everything: who needed surgery or stitches, drugs or tests, X-rays or stomach pumps. Even who lived or died. There were tall doctors, short doctors, dishy doctors, ugly doctors, fat and thin doctors, bushy-haired doctors, bald doctors, experienced and rookie doctors, good and bad and indifferent, young and old. You got yourself sick or injured and you took whatever was available.

Dr. David Blume was about average. He was thirty, dark and good-looking, efficient without being brilliant, five foot eleven and too skinny. He was kind and thoughtful to his patients without seeming smarmy, patronizing or over-sentimental. Up on the tenth floor, Dr. Blume was setting off on his evening rounds. He had grabbed a quick coffee from the machine in the reception foyer and, while he was drinking it, checked over the list of the most recent admissions. Then he'd taken the elevator up to the tenth and stepped into a corridor through a door marked WOMEN'S SURGICAL. The white, amorphous ghost of his surgeon's gown, reflected from the high-gloss of the white-painted walls, flitted along silently beside him down the wide passageway. As he strode along, he casually glanced at the numbers on the doors to the wards. Outside WS104 he paused. The door was slightly ajar.

As always, he rapped politely on the wooden paneling

before entering. Despite his several years' residence at the hospital, he still felt the need for a modicum of polite formality, especially when entering the wards of women patients. You never knew what you might catch them doing, if you simply barged right in. One time he'd walked into a women's ward without knocking and had found a thirty-six-year-old woman patient providing an unsolicited urine sample, right there in the middle of the floor. She was a psychiatric case who'd needed surgery and he'd been fairly new to the job and, despite all he'd seen in medical school, and he'd experienced during his stint as an intern, he had been surprised, to put it mildly. What the woman had been using as a receptacle for the urine sample was a size-nine, high-heeled shoe which, as anyone will tell you, is not really satisfactory. So he always knocked.

As usual, nobody answered, so he stepped inside and looked around. Mrs. Marie Rosella was sitting up in bed, supported by a barricade of pillows, freshly changed and dazzling white under the fluorescent lighting. She was just sitting there, her hands gently clasped in her lap, knees slightly raised, eyes half closed, looking at nothing. Next to her in the small, two-bed ward, a young girl was lying on her side, head propped on her hand, tapping the fingers of her other hand gently on the turned-down bedclothes in time with the beat of music coming from a portable stereo cassette machine which lay on the table beside her bed.

Mrs. Rosella did not move from her rigid, propped-up position as Dr. Blume entered, but when her eyes moved languidly towards the door and she saw him, a faint welcoming smile of recognition spread across her pale lips. Intravenous tubes snaked down to each of her sinewy, sallow skinned arms from drip-feed bottles, suspended on their chromium tubular frames on either side of the bed. Dr. Blume stepped forward and bent over her.

"Mrs. Rosella," he said. "Comesta?"

He gently brushed her cheek with his lips. She looked over-tired and world-weary, yet the fine bone structure that almost showed through the lined, waxen texture of her skin, still affirmed that she had once been an attractive woman.

Dr. Blume glanced at the other patient to see if she was listening, but her eyes were closed as she continued her tattoo with her fingers in time to the music. He turned back to Mrs. Rosella and half whispered, conspiratorially:

"Did you bring any of my favorite Fettuccini?"

She had not, in fact, had time before being admitted to prepare some of the pasta that she had brought for Dr. Blume on the last two occasions. But she ignored the question. She was too busy eyeing him carefully, as if she were the doctor and he the patient.

"You don' look well," Mrs. Rosella said in the New York-Italian accent that she would never lose, even if she lived for another sixty-eight years. She said it with genuine concern, her face puckered into an admonishing look, as if at any moment she would cluck her tongue and shake her head disapprovingly. Dr. Blume smiled inwardly. Italian mamas, they were all the same. Just like Jewish ones. Always married too young, raised too many kids, loved them too much and worked and worried too hard. You could say they lived so intensively they killed themselves doing it.

"You not eating?" she asked, frowning at him.

"You tell them old Marie is back and they should feed you good, eh?"

All the time she was speaking, her eyes wandering, probingly, over his face, Dr. Blume was doing his own stock-taking on his patient. And at the same time, he was trying to avoid telegraphing anything of his own concern for her. She did not look terribly strong. Would she, he wondered, be able to stand up to the considerable surgery she would need this time? It was touch and go. This would be the fourth op. in three years and she had bronchial asthma and emphysema. He would have to have a talk with Dr Howard, the lung specialist and try to make sure they got one of the best anesthetists— Seltzer, or Larry Packmann. Mrs. Rosella was still scrutinizing him. She reached out a bony wrist and touched his cheek with her calloused fingertips.

"And you' face," she said. "Something…I don't know. You' hair. Why you losing you' hair? Such a handsome young boy…"

And he was handsome, almost in a classical sense. Fine, unlined features, balanced jawline, a straight nose that was not too narrow, high cheekbones and a mouth that was full-lipped without being effeminate. Yet his hair…

He raised a hand to his brow self-consciously as she spoke, tracing his fingers along the obviously fast-receding hairline. His eyes took on a strange, faraway glaze as he pondered what Mrs. Rosella had said. So others were beginning to notice now…. Then he recovered himself. She was still waiting for him to say something.

"Uh…too much aggravation, I guess," he shrugged with a nervous grin. Then he flashed her a warm smile; not a switched-on-bedside-manner smile, but a genuine signal of friendliness.

"My patients aren't all sweeties like you," he said. He straightened up and stepped to the foot of the bed and unhooked the clipboard progress chart that was hanging on the bed frame. He glanced over it thoughtfully for a moment, alternately darting quick looks at his patient, then rehooked it on the rail.

"You try to sleep now, eh?" he said, smiling again and winking at her. He turned to the girl in the other bed and, with a scarcely noticeable flutter of his delicate surgeon's fingers, signaled her to turn down the cassette machine. The girl reached over to the low night table and complied, lowering the volume to an almost inaudible level.

Dr. Blume turned back to his patient, raising an eyebrow with an expression that silently repeated his question. Was she going to be a good bambino and try to get some rest?

"Only if you give me a little more Demerol," Mrs. Rosella said.

He smiled his assent. A few tranquilizers would be okay, she needed—deserved, even—the rest. Her eyebrows, which had not turned silver like her long, straight hair, but were sharply defined and jet black, creased into the ghost of a frown. Her face pantomimed the wheedling expression of a little girl.

"You gonna cut me up again, Doctor?"

The way he was looking at her, she knew he was. But he did not have the heart to nod or to give her any other conscious sign of affirmation. He blinked slowly and smiled again. His expression once more repeated his request. The rest? Was she going to try to sleep? She looked at him for a moment then closed her eyes obediently. And in that brief instant before she did so, her own expression told him that she knew she'd have to have surgery again.

He turned and went out of the ward, gently closing the door behind him.

In the other wards of the sprawling great hospital, this miniature city within a city, there were thousands more patients, other people, other lives. And he was responsible for a sizeable share of them, once they were booked into the operating theater. And out there, beyond the hospital walls, were millions more, lining up, aching and dying and falling over each other, stabbing and beating and stomping each other, waiting for their turn to come in. A whole city full of them. Enough to make anyone lose his hair, even at thirty.

CHAPTER 2

THE COLOR TELEVISION in Apartment 202, 1146 West Comox, twenty stories above the heart of the Bronx, was switched on and the volume was at a moderate level. But for the moment, nobody was watching. Not really. Not Wendy Flemming, not little Samantha Andretti, nor her little brother, Jason.

Normally, Wendy had it switched on from morning until night and occasionally she watched. The rest of the time it was background noise "just for company." Yet even when she had company, like tonight, it was still left on. But neither she nor her company were watching. Oh, occasionally one of them would glance up at the screen for a few seconds, then look away. But that wasn't what you could call watching. That was like glancing at the clock to see what time it was, or to check if the damned thing was still running.

No, what they were doing tonight, what Wendy was doing, at least, was reading a bedtime story. Well, half-reading, half-improvising, to tell the truth. Wendy had the book open on her lap and sometimes she read from it, pointing to the words, one by one, finger-reading. And other times she just looked up straight ahead and made bits up as she went along. And what Samantha and her brother were doing, some of the time, anyway, was listening. Samantha was snuggled right beside

Wendy on the long sofa. She was the best listener. She paid attention, most of the time, hardly even glancing up at the TV screen at all. Next to Samantha was Jason and, well, he wasn't quite such an attentive listener. He had this teddy bear on his knee and sometimes he listened and sometimes he looked up at the TV when a particularly bright picture caught his attention, and other times he fiddled about with the teddy. Sometimes he was fiddling and listening. Sometimes he was watching the TV and listening. Sometimes he was even fiddling and watching and listening. But only a little of the time was he just listening. He was only two-and-a-half. What can you expect?

So there they were the three of them, partly into a bedtime story, all cozy and with the bright colors of the TV screen reflecting on their shiny faces as they snuggled together on the sofa, in Wendy's apartment.

Wendy pushed gently at her long brown hair, which at present was tied up in a neat pile on top of her head in a sort of lop-sided cone. Then, satisfied that it was in place, she felt around the nape of her neck and found a wisp that was astray. She deftly tucked it in and looked down again to the open storybook on her lap to find where she was up to.

"So…the next day, the handsome prince came to the castle and called up to the princess," she resumed.

"'Rapunzel, Rapunzel, let down your hair'"

Jason, who had had one of his lapses and had been momentarily mesmerized by the television picture, suddenly realized he was missing out on some of the story. So he shouted:

"And then WHAAAAAAT!"

At the top of his lungs. Wendy cringed and shook her shoulders and at the same time nervously clutched at the collar of her apricot housecoat.

"Hey, quiet down, kiddo!" she snapped. "My head's killing me." Jason looked at her, all saucer eyed and innocent. She ignored him.

"So then the princess untied her long, long hair and dropped it out of the window," she resumed once more.

"Why?" Jason wanted to know.

"Listen, kiddo," Wendy said, getting a shade rattled. "You want to hear this or don't you?" Then, almost to herself, she added: "I think I'll charge your mother extra for storytelling. It's not in my contract."

Nestling beside Wendy, Samantha was also beginning to find her brother's interruptions tiresome.

"Quiet, Jason," she said, indignantly. "Go ahead, Wendy."

Fine, thought Wendy. Here am I supposed to be baby-sitting and I'm getting orders from a four-year-old kid. She forced a sickly smile and said:

"Right on, sister." She didn't bother to consult the storybook anymore. What was the use? She might as well have had Macy's catalogue in her lap for all the kids cared.

"Anyway," she ad-libbed, "this prince is a little weird, ya know, and likes to climb on hairy ladders. So... he grabs onto Rapunzel's hair and starts to climb up to the tower..."

Just at that moment something on the television triggered a feeling of familiarity in Wendy's head.

Like when a person can hear his own name mentioned over the hubbub of a dozen other conversations all going on at once. She glanced up and stared at the screen and her eyes widened, unblinkingly, as though she was in a trance.

On the screen was a paid political announcement. There was a film of a handsome man in his early thirties, moving slowly through a street lined with people. His left thumb was hooked in the hanger-tab of his jacket, which he carried draped over his shoulder. From time to time he darted out his right hand to grasp and shake warmly the extended hands of people in the crowd. Despite his casual approach, he had style and class. He had a kind of young executive air about him: a go-getter charisma. His teeth flashed in a warm, eager, go-ahead smile. His hair was dark brown and well-groomed, not too short, not too long, a sort of no-nonsense compromise between straight and hip, trimmed and shaped neatly to lie over the tops of his ears.

As the film rolled, the chocolate-syrup voice of an announcer's dubbed-over commentary was in progress.

The announcer was saying: "…in the nineteen-sixties, Edward Flemming and his generation shook the establishment with new ideas and values. As a congressman he can continue by working within the system for the future…"

Wendy was still gazing intently at the screen, the kids and the story totally forgotten as a horde of memories and images flooded back to her, like some action replay gone berserk. On the one hand, she was remembering warmer, fonder times; on the other she was thinking: The creep! What a bullshitter—the bastard!

Samantha's excited voice suddenly brought Wendy back to her present surroundings.

"Wendy! Hey, Wendy! That's Mr. Flemming, Wendy? Mr. Flemming's on TV!"

Samantha's blue eyes darted about, from Wendy, to the TV screen, to her baby brother who did not seem in the least interested or impressed, then back to Wendy again. Jason was engaged in an intensive study of his teddy bear's torn ear.

On the screen Edward Flemming was still pumping hands in the street, vote-catching and exchanging pleasantries with his supporters. He shook hands with an old man and flashed a grin at the camera as if to say: See? I may be young and trendy and hip, but I've got time for all you old folks, too.

Wendy glanced at Samantha and said vaguely: "Mr. Flemming is running for Congress."

She looked thoughtfully back at the television and added:

"Maybe some day he'll even be President." And she was thinking: He will, too, the bastard.

Samantha's eyes widened even more and her mouth shaped itself into a surprised and highly impressed "O" of wonder. Her breath came in tiny, excited gasps and she was barely able to stop her words tumbling over each other.

"An'…an'…an' you'll live in the White House an' we can come and visit?"

Wendy smiled wearily and looked at the wonderstruck kid beside her. She ruffled Samantha's hair playfully with one hand.

"I'm afraid not, kiddo," she said, with a trace of laconic weariness. Then, seeing the child's puzzled expression, she added:

"Mr. Flemming and I aren't…uh…living together anymore."

First Samantha looked incredulous, then indignant.

"But he's your husband!" she protested, as if that solved everything.

Wendy wasn't listening. She had turned back to watch the screen again. The political plug was ending on a freeze-shot of Edward Flemming's handsome features in tight close-up. And the announcer was urging:

"Put Edward Flemming in Congress!"

And Wendy was thinking: Put him a concrete suit in the Hudson.

"Edward Flemming *is* the future!" the announcer insisted.

Not my goddamn future, Wendy thought.

Goddamn him! She tried to remember the earlier, happier times, of their first meeting, their warmth, their romance, their marriage. But it didn't work. Everything had come unglued and Edward Flemming was just a bitter taste in her mouth.

Jason's high, piping, insistent voice broke in on her reverie.

"Tell about the hair ladder!" he demanded. "An'…an'…Rap-pun-zel." He had trouble pronouncing the oddly alien name of Grimm Brothers' vintage.

Samantha thought that was a good idea, too, and chimed in. "Yeah…tell us, Wendy!"

Wendy gathered her thoughts, put Edward Flemming in the irretrievably past catalogue, glanced briefly at the two children and resumed.

"Right," she said. "The hair ladder. So...the prince grabs onto Rapunzel's hair and starts to climb up to the tower."

She clenched her hands before her as if she were grasping a thick rope, pantomiming the prince's climb for the kids. Jason got the message quickly.

"I wanna do it! I wanna do it!" he yelled, roughly flinging the forlorn teddy bear on one side in his excitement and reaching out towards Wendy. For a brief instant, she thought he wanted to go to the bathroom in a hurry and she was about to grab him and make a dash for it. Then she realized what he meant. She sighed. Ah well, anything for peace and quiet. She reached up and unfastened her long, straight brown hair that cascaded silkenly down her back to a point halfway between her shoulder blades and her waist. She leaned over, inclining her head towards Jason, allowing her tresses to fall within the grasp of his pudgy pink hands. He seized a couple of tot-sized fistfuls and began to heave, trying to tug himself up onto his feet on the seat of the sofa beside her. Samantha got a little crushed during the operation. The torn teddy bear lay sad and pathetic on the arm of the couch. "Ouch!" Wendy yelled, but she was only kidding.

She gave Jason even more play on her hair by leaning further over towards him. Samantha got even more squashed. Jason went on tugging.

"Hey, kiddo," she joked, "if you want to get into the castle that bad, there's a secret staircase around the side—"

At that moment Jason yanked even harder and kicked out with his stubby little legs.

"Ouch!" This time Wendy wasn't kidding. "Hey! That's enough!" she squealed. "Lay off now, brother!"

Jason thought it was hilarious and kept a tight hold, still tugging furiously at her hair. With her head still tilted uncomfortably to one side, Wendy grappled around, trying to find his hands and pry them off her hair. Jason leaned back like a stevedore doing the old yo-heave-ho routine. Then, suddenly, Wendy was free. At first she thought Jason had let go, but when she straightened up and looked at him, his tiny paws were still clutching long hanks of her lovely locks. He was giggling hysterically, waving the hair. Then he threw it at her. Wendy caught it and straightened it out in her lap, examining it curiously. Instead of having broken off, entire long strands had come out at the very roots.

The two children fell silent as, with one hand, Wendy reached gingerly up and tenderly felt around for the place where her hair had so easily come adrift. Her eyes were still watering slightly from the sharp stab of pain when Jason tugged out her hair. Her fingers felt carefully around and, eventually, she located the spot. There was no blood. But there was a small, but quite definite, bare patch on the left side of her head, high up towards her center parting.

Jesus, she thought. I'm going goddamn bald!

CHAPTER 3

THERE WAS a look of utter hopelessness and despair on Barbara O'Malley's face as she clutched at her coffee mug and sat at the kitchen table across from her visitor. It was also a look that reached out, pleading or demanding something; comfort, reassurance or advice of some kind. But Richie Grosso did not know what to say, where to begin. He sipped his coffee and gazed blankly back at his next-door neighbor.

She was only in her late twenties and still attractive. But the look of worry that had recently become almost a permanent fixture, etched across her face, made her seem a lot older. The large, dark eyes were showing signs of strain and sleeplessness and they bore the beginnings of worry lines around them and bags beneath them. The corners of her pretty, bow-shaped mouth had begun to turn down and sag and it wouldn't be long before there were tell-tale lines of stress permanently engraved there, too.

She sighed. It was domestic trouble, as usual. "Maybe he should quit the Force," she said, resignedly. "At least I'd get to see him once in a while…" But her voice trailed off in a dearth of enthusiasm, an absence of any faith in her own judgement.

Richie's large German Shepherd dog, unimaginatively yet

aptly named Shep, stirred sleepily at his feet where it lay sprawled, half under the kitchen table.

"No, Barbara," Richie said, fixing her with his gaze. "That's the worst thing he can do."

He waved an arm vaguely in the direction of the open door to the living room. Music was drifting in from a stereo player. There was a rich, rhythmic bass-line and a bank of gently rocking strings, punctuated by brass. Over the top was a deep, dark brown male voice. And Richie thought: Barry White, current droolsville hero of the bored suburban housewife.

"He'd wind up sitting around the house with his face in the bottle from morning till night," Richie said, still riveting Barbara with his steady, steel grey gaze. Barbara sighed again and looked down at her hands. She did not nod her agreement, but Richie could see that she knew he was right.

Just then two young boys burst in from the living room and, without even glancing at their mother or her neighbor, headed straight for the tall refrigerator in the corner. Johnny, the younger of the two, had a vividly-colored macaw perched on his shoulder. Its plumage was dominated by strikingly rich blues and greens. As Johnny opened the 'fridge door and reached inside, the parrot blinked, readjusted its grip on his shoulder and began grooming its breast feathers with a large, grey curved beak.

Barbara looked up, seeing what her son was raiding from the 'fridge.

"No, Johnny!" she barked suddenly. "No more chocolate pudding! That one's for your father!"

Startled by the suddenness and violence of his mother's outburst, Johnny quickly placed the pudding back on the shelf of the 'fridge. He closed the door and, turning, shrugged his shoulders at his brother, Kevin. The elder of Barbara's sons gave a quick jerk of his head towards the living room door and, without a word, the boys trooped sheepishly out of the kitchen.

Barbara's hand trembled slightly as she reached for her

coffee mug. She hadn't meant to be so sharp with the boy; it had just happened, she couldn't help it. Her nerves were in tatters. Richie had noticed. She breathed in deeply, trying to compose herself, but was unable. Tears welled in her eyes as she glanced up at the battery-powered clock on the kitchen wall and she had to blink to focus. The clock resolved itself from its watery blur. It was 11:30 p.m. She looked across at Richie.

"Oh, Richie," she said with an involuntary intake of breath that was half gasp, half sob. "I don't know what to do any more." She could feel the tears about to overflow her lower lids again and blinked them back with another deep breath.

"Look at me," she said, holding out a trembling hand. "I'm a wreck. I feel like an old woman."

Once more she sighed and her shoulders sagged despairingly.

"Maybe it's my fault…"

Her voice trailed off on a note of utter despair.

Richie leaned forward in his chair, drumming the table emphatically with his fist as he spoke.

"Your fault?" he echoed. "Look, Barbara—he goes to work at seven in the morning and you don't hear from him till midnight. Then he comes home crocked out of his brain."

He shook his head slowly, drawing in breath between clenched teeth. He felt almost as exasperated as he knew she must feel. After all, what could he, or Barbara, or anyone do? Barbara started off on a fresh tack, and, almost before she began to speak, Richie knew it would still be on the defensive for her husband, apologetic and self-effacing.

"Maybe it's the strain," she said. "He's been having these awful nightmares. Sometimes, being a cop…"

"Barbara, *please*," Richie cut her off. "Save the cop bullshit, huh? Believe me, cops don't work that hard." He drew a hand around his jaw, as if checking for late-night stubble. She was about to speak again, but he cut in quickly.

"And I know all about that hair," he said. He flourished a

hand in the air beside his temple. "What is he—the only person that ever lost his hair?" he said, sarcastically. I've been losing a couple of strands lately, too, you know. But that ain't no excuse. You know what I mean?"

He snorted derisively.

"Huh! I think you deserve better, that's all..."

But his final word trailed on the air and the forcefulness suddenly drained from Richie's voice. His face froze, his jaw sagging open.

There, behind Barbara, framed in the open kitchen doorway, still wearing his heavy winter coat, stood Barbara's husband, John O'Malley. Richie's mind began to race. How much had he heard? Was he juiced out of his brain as usual? What would he say, or perhaps even worse, do? As the questions piled up unspoken and for the time being unanswered, Richie tried to relax his expression to a friendly, but not altogether sincere, smile and at the same time tried to figure out what state O'Malley was in. The cop's face was flushed red, but that could simply have been the biting February cold. The eyes: you could usually tell by the eyes. They were somewhat glazed, the upper lids drooping slightly. How long had he been standing there? Or maybe just outside the open door to the kitchen? There was no way of telling. And O'Malley's face was practically inscrutable, although it bore the faintest trace of knowing contempt.

Richie finally managed to force a grin and spoke. "Hey, John."

But the words caught in his throat and the tall policeman did not reply. He simply stood there, his face immobile, giving little away except a hint that he had been drinking. How much was hard to tell.

Richie glanced at John's hair. It was long and full yet had the strange, artificial look of a shop window dummy, as if it had been brushed carefully into place, then quick-frozen with lacquer so that it would not change its position or shape.

Slowly, sluggishly, O'Malley's glassy stare turned upon his wife then, uncertainly, back to Richie. Then he began to move. For a fleeting moment, Richie thought he was going to strike Barbara, but O'Malley moved behind her, heading for the refrigerator in the corner. He swung open the large door, leaning on it slightly for support, reached inside and drew out a can of chilled beer. At that moment, the younger O'Malley boy, Johnny, appeared in the lounge doorway and stared across at his father, who was once more stooping, leaning into the 'fridge. O'Malley was removing the chocolate pudding, as well as the beer.

The blue and green macaw was still perched on young Johnny's shoulder, but when it caught sight of the familiar, stocky figure over by the 'fridge, it suddenly gave a flurry with its wings and awkwardly flapped the few yards across the room to perch on the shoulder of Johnny's father.

"Hello, Johnny, hello!" it squawked in O'Malley Senior's ear, darting its head from side to side with characteristic jerkiness. John O'Malley, clutching his can of beer and carton of chocolate pudding to his chest with one arm, shoved the refrigerator door closed, turned and marched out of the room, past Barbara, past his son Johnny, past Richie and his dog, without looking at any of them, without uttering a single word.

Richie saw his cue.

"Well," he said, with a feigned yawn that he hoped didn't seem too artificial. "C'mon, Shep. Time to hit the sack."

He got up from the table, flashing a brief, weak smile at Barbara. He hoped it said something; he hoped it reached into the void that had settled around his unfortunate neighbor and gave her comfort, even if only a microscopic, gentle pat on the back, of reassurance. But somehow, he knew it did not. What the hell could he say? Thanks for the coffee? It was all so strained, so futile.

As he made his way out the door and down the drive towards his own detached suburban home in the neatly landscaped development of Valley Stream, New York, he wondered vaguely what would transpire back in the O'Malley house. Would Barbara get a beating for entertaining a male neighbor while her husband was out? Would the abyss that had slowly opened between John and Barbara O'Malley continue to gape and grow until they were worlds apart? What would become of those two fine boys?

He felt certain of only one thing: whatever happened in the future, the O'Malley place would always be a house, a pleasant, middle-class suburban, American house like millions of others. But it would never be a home.

CHAPTER 4

It turned out to be one hell of a party. There were just the eight of them—nine when Frannie showed up later—all around the same age, give or take a year or two, late twenties, early thirties, all too intent on having a ball to be bothered by the cold. And anyway, there was a roaring log blaze in the red brick fireplace and the ski house was a mile or so from town, so they could make all the goddamn noise they liked. And they liked, this crowd, once they got started.

Tony was there, Tony Rocco, and he was always a riot. Then there was Tommy and Joe and Jerry and the four chicks, all well into the sauce. All warm and pleasantly oiled and out of the spiky February chill, up there in the pinewood country ski house on the snowy slopes of Hillsdale, upstate New York. Jerry —Jerry Zipkin—had brought his tenor sax and was sprawled on the floor, legs spread out, his back against an armchair, playing a drooling, quiet improvisation, breathing sexily into the reed, pretending he was Stan Getz during his Brazilian bossa nova period or something. Actually, he looked more like Gerry Mulligan with his neat, close-cropped, college boy haircut, but Mulligan is a baritone, not a tenor man.

Jerry was between jobs—he was a college lecturer—and his

sax playing was good enough to keep him in pocket money playing private gigs. They used to call him Jerry Zipgun at high school, although he'd never carried one; it was just the sound of his name, Zipkin. Some of the kids called him Zipgun, others plumped for Zipper or Zippy.

He was pretty zippy, too, always rushing around a lot, too many things to do, striding about on those long legs, head thrust forward eagerly, carrying six books he was reading all at one time and his battered tenor case.

At the party, Jerry's services came free. He was playing for love, not money. His girlfriend, Alicia, was sitting beside him, knees up to her chin, her face against the shoulder of his fraying Banion shirt, her eyes closed, getting lost in the music. She was a stunning looker, Alicia, with indigo eyes shaped like walnut shells and long, flowing, raven black hair. You couldn't tell, the way she was sitting, all hunched up, or in the clothes she was wearing, the loose blouse and denim bolero jacket and flared jeans, but she was well stacked, too.

The rest of the gang were standing, sitting, or slouching around the cabin, drinks in hand, talking and laughing. There was big Joe Trezza, a husky, square-shouldered guy of about twenty-eight, looking like an ex-prize fighter who had been reluctantly crammed into a suit, standing with his girl, Margaret, a laughing-eyed redhead. They stood face to face, foreheads almost touching, gazing at each other over the rims of their glasses, as if there was no one else around.

Backs to the fireplace, heads bowed in some heavy conversation, something about a new exhibition at the Freer Gallery, stood Tommy Ellison and his girl, Francine. Tommy always looked amazingly hip with his early-Dylan head of curls and Zapata-style moustache, a black sweatshirt under a leather vest, one hand hooked by the thumb in the seat pocket of his Levi's. Francine, who had long, auburn hair, leaned her ear towards him as he rattled on about Oriental art.

Tony Rocco came back from the bathroom, looked around at the gathering impishly, and prepared to go into action. He climbed up onto one of the two spacious, chunky armchairs with the faded beige seat covers, placing his feet on the wide arms, and clambered up onto the backrest. Arms outstretched as he tried to keep his balance, he turned awkwardly to face into the room, squatting there like some gigantic, grotesque bird, holding out the edges of his open-fronted Cowichan Indian sweater, as if they were wings.

Alicia opened her eyes, saw him across the room and nudged Jerry. He stopped playing his sax and looked across, thinking: What's the crazy son-of-a-bitch up to now?

Tony perched there, pulling a peculiar face with his flexible, rubbery features, his lips pursed like a funnel, his eyes staring, head darting about jerkily on his scrawny neck. Tommy and Francine, over by the fireplace, also noticed what was going on and stopped talking to watch.

Tommy smiled slowly behind his hand as he dabbed tiny drops of his drink from his full moustache with a tissue. He turned to Francine and pointed a finger at the perching Tony.

"Watch this. You remember Rodan?"

"The artist? Francine asked, looking puzzled. Because they'd been talking art, she thought That was who he'd meant naturally.

Tommy laughed.

"No—the monster," he said. He'd seen this part of Tony's act before.

Tony slowly began to flap his arms, still holding

onto the edges of his sweater, as he crouched gawkishly on his haunches on the back of the armchair. It, was a remarkably accurate mime of Rodan, the giant, reptilian bird from the Japanese horror film classic of the 'fifties. Rodan, the gigantic pterodactyl who had lain dormant in his colossal egg inside a mountain for millions of years, until he was incubated and hatched out by the heat from a volcanic eruption. Whereupon, he promptly flew off and demolished Tokyo. Just like that. Well, it was only to be expected after such a rude awakening.

Tony-Rodan's beady, hawk-hooded eyes ranged around the room, looking at each of them as if trying to decide which one to devour first. Then he began to utter high-pitched, birdlike screeches: AWWWWRRRRRK! AWWWWWWRRRRRK! And his wings flapped faster and faster as he poised for takeoff.

The guys were already chuckling at Tony's fantastic talent for mimicry, even though some of them had seen it before. But one or two of the girls didn't look too certain; they looked mesmerized, or worried, or both. And that made the guys laugh even more. Alicia bit into her little finger. Francine coughed nervously and thought: Is he crazy? Tina marveled at how the guy managed to keep his balance up there on the chair back, beating his arms wildly as he did so. Margaret thought: Is he...is he really going to...?

And yes, he was. Suddenly, with an ear-rending screech, Tony leapt up into the air from his perch, bounding down onto the arms of the chair, then onto the cushioned seat, then off and around the room, still shrieking and flapping his wings wildly. Chairs went flying, ashtrays scattered their contents, drinks were spilled as hands swiftly retracted to avoid the whirlwind passage of the insane monster, and the girls backed into corners nervously, wishing Rodan would change back into just plain old Tony again and restore some semblance of sanity.

All the same, they all laughed hysterically as the strange, angular creature that Tony had become squawked and flapped and hopped and leapt and roared about the room, like a cross between a badly-designed, enraged ostrich and Jerry Lewis doing one of his spastic routines.

It was shaping up to be one hell of a party, for sure.

After a while, though, the Invasion of Rodan II became too much. That was often Tony's trouble. He didn't know when to quit.

Breathless, dizzied and semi-hysterical himself from his wild whirling assault on the room, Tony staggered violently into Joe Trezza, slamming against his arm and sending his drink flying. Some of the Scotch and soda that Joe had been sipping splashed on the sleeve of his wine-colored suit jacket. The glass continued on to the hearth, where it shattered.

"Hey!" Joe bellowed and aimed a straight left at Tony. It caught him hard on the shoulder, knocking him sideways, sprawling to the floor and bringing the saga of the Return of Rodan to an abrupt close.

"This is a Pierre Cardin," Joe said, indignantly, brushing ineffectively at his stained sleeve with his hand. "Cost me two-and-a-half!"

"You hurt him, Joe," Francine said, looking concernedly down at Tony, who lay spreadeagled, or rather spread-pterodactyled, on the thick woolly rug.

"Hurt him?" Joe snarled, "I'll kill him."

But he was smiling as he snarled. As Tony sat up, shaking his head, trying to struggle to his feet, Joe faked another punch at him, but pulled it, about four inches from Tony's jaw. Then he put out a ham of a hand to help Tony up.

"You all right, you crazy bastard?" Joe laughed.

Breathless, Tony nodded, looking up at Joe, who towered a good five inches above him. Then he narrowed his eyes and, in a heavily exaggerated, Hollywood-Japanese accent, said:

"Ah. So you think you kill monster. Not so, Charlie. That was only baby. The mother come...ten times size. Kill you and all Tokyo..."

Everybody hooted with half-drunken laughter. You could always count on old Tony to come back with a punchline. Okay, maybe it wasn't that funny, but it seemed that way with everybody half gassed. As the laughter subsided, Jerry began playing his sax again, trying to make like Stan Getz, circa 1964. A buzz of relaxed conversation resumed. Yeah, a hell of a party.

Jerry was warming into *Corcovado* and Francine, Tommy's

date began moving gently to the music as she and Tommy talked; not dancing, just shuffling her feet and swaying her hips to the soft bossa nova rhythm where she stood.

Tina, a chic, blackberry-eyed little Italian who was Tony's girl, threw back her head and laughed delightedly, all white teeth and cute dimples, at one of his jokes.

Alicia snuggled down again next to Jerry, dreaming, her eyes closed, as he went on with the Brazilian jazz samba.

After the broken glass had been cleaned away by Margaret and the upset chairs and ashtrays restored to their original positions, the outer door to the ski house opened and a brief, icy draught preceded a late arrival. Frannie Scott came in through the small entrance hall, his feet ringing on the pine flooring. There was a chorus of cheers and how-are-ya's and so-you-finally-made-it as Frannie stood grinning in the doorway to the party room, an expensive Hasselblad camera with a flash attachment and a power pack slung around his neck. Frannie was a suave, urbane, handsome-looking guy who always managed to give the impression, the way he dressed, that he was on his way to or from a nightclub.

While all the handshaking and backslapping was going on, Margaret started mixing Frannie a martini. But when she edged her way through the small cluster of people around him to hand him the drink, he was clapping his hands and ushering people away over towards the picture-window set in one wall of the room.

"Okay, everybody!" Frannie shouted. "Let's line up for a group shot." As he spoke, he removed the lens cap from his camera and switched on his battery pack to make sure it was charging.

But Tommy Ellison stepped forward, holding up a palm and shaking his head, like one of those people outside theaters and courtrooms and tribunals who say: "No publicity."

"Frankie-boy," Tommy said. "Do *My Way* first."

My Way was Frannie's party piece, the way it was the party piece of just about everybody in the world who thought they could sing. There's one in every crowd and they always sing it as if it were written for them, personally. Sometimes they make a good job of it, sometimes they louse it up with histrionics. Frannie was not bad. Not Sinatra by a long stretch, but okay. The gang cheered and egged him on.

"Yeah, come on, Frannie—do it for us!" Tina chirped, clapping her hands.

At first, Frannie mirrored Tommy's upraised palm and shook his head modestly. But they all kept on at him and at length he lifted the camera and powerpack straps from around his neck and looked about for somewhere safe to stash his equipment.

"Okay, okay," he said. "I'll do it. But I need my back-up. Where's Jerry?"

Jerry, who by now had resumed his place, squatting on the floor, hunched his shoulders and tried to wriggle off behind the armchair, embarrassed. But Alicia was tugging at his elbow and one of the other girls came over and started pulling him to his feet by the armpits. Slowly and reluctantly, Jerry allowed himself to be raised, looking nervously around, clutching his tenor to his chest. He tried to sit down again, but Joe grabbed him by the shoulders and lifted him to his feet. Then he took hold of the neck of the sax and the back of Jerry's head and guided the mouthpiece towards his lips.

Tony, always fanatical for authenticity and atmosphere, went over and cut the cabin lights, except for a chrome table lamp, which he swiveled around until its beam fell on Frannie like a spotlight, just like they do in the clubs. Happier now that he could not be properly seen, out beyond the perimeter of the lamp's beam, Jerry began to blow an introductory few bars of the song. As he did so, Frannie reached up and loosened his shirt collar buttons, his back to the audience. He lit a cigarette and picked up the martini that Margaret had mixed for him, then turned and stepped into the center of the improvised spot.

He really turned it on, then, Frannie. Just like he was booked at the Coconut Grove or the Sands in Las Vegas. With his drink and cigarette in one hand, he wandered around the room, singing, with Jerry's sax all breathy and sexy, mooning along behind him, pausing for effect on particular passages, looking up at an imaginary gallery, then down at the girls who sat and stood around in a tight circle, listening. As he meandered among them, Tony followed him with the spotlight, swiveling the lamp around. Occasionally, Frannie leaned forward to take one of the girls' hands, or to peck teasingly at her lips. The girls played along, sighing and murmuring, "Oh, Frankie!"

At one point Alicia decided to feign a swoon and, as she almost fell over sideways, realized how drunk she was becoming.

Frannie, meanwhile, wallowed in all the mock adulation. It was almost like the old days when they swooned over Sinatra in Times Square, or screamed themselves silly for Johnny Ray at the London Palladium. Almost, but not quite. And all the time, Frannie crooned on, really hamming it, squeezing everything he could out of each syllable, every gesture.

What bugged Joe was when Frannie stepped forward and, during a pause in the verse, planted a long, lingering kiss full on the lips of Margaret, Joe's girl. Joe's eyes narrowed and he felt himself tense as the jealousy welled up inside him. He studied Frannie closely as he moved off, continuing the song. Something—he hadn't quite decided what—was odd about Frannie tonight. Then, as Frannie half-turned, serenading Alicia, Joe saw what it was.

The song was just about drawing to its climax. Joe pushed forward, elbowing his way through the small knot of people who stood listening in the darkness. He stepped into the spot-light, directly in front of Frannie.

"Just a minute," he said, cutting in on Frannie's singing. "What's this?"

And before Frannie could move, Joe reached out and grabbed his hair, pulling at it. There was a gasp from everybody in the gang as the whole head of hair came away in Joe's hand: a full hairpiece. Underneath, standing there in the bright white glare of the lamp, Frannie froze, his mouth open, his head completely bald, reflecting the single bulb of the table lamp. His eyes stared wide, horror-stricken, almost like those of a zombie. Then he moved.

Like a striking cobra his hand darted out and grabbed the wig from Joe and he turned, frantically trying to put the hairpiece back in place on his bald pate, tugging desperately at it, trying to get it straight. Then, turning his back on all of them, he dashed out of the room, out the front door of the cabin and off into the night.

For an instant, they all stood around, dumbfounded, squinting incredulously at each other in the muted light from the fire, barely able to believe what they had seen. Joe was the first to speak.

"What the hell happened to his hair?" he said, open-mouthed, still extending the hand that had held Frannie's wig.

"I don't know," Tommy said, looking around at each of the half-lit faces in turn. "Did you see that?"

"Like a cue ball!" Joe said, shaking his head. "Hey, Jerry, you should know. Why'd he shave his head?"

Jerry spread his hands, palms upwards, letting his sax dangle on its cord around his neck.

"It's news to me," he said.

Alicia, still feeling very woozy from all the drink, was leaning on Jerry, clutching his arm for support.

Just then a tall, white, amorphous figure appeared in the shadows by the door to the cabin bedroom. One of the girls screamed, pointing, as the ghostly white, shrouded figure moved slowly towards them, head bowed, face hooded and shadowed like a monk. Everybody froze.

The figure kept coming. Then, as it stood among them, the head lifted, and Tony's sardonic grin appeared beneath the cowl, blinking into the light with a mad, wide-eyed expression.

"Who's got two quarters?" he said, grinning maniacally and thrusting a clawed, grasping hand out from beneath the folds of the bedsheet, like a beggar seeking alms. Joe's girl, Margaret, fumbled in her purse for a second, then held out two quarters, dropping them into Tony's upturned palm.

He turned his back for a moment, rummaging about within the sheet. Then, stooping low, twisting his body crookedly, he wheeled around like a demented hunchback. He had placed the two shiny coins over each of his eyes, holding them in place with his face muscles, like monocles. It was a grim and bizarre sight in the subdued light, as if a corpse had come back to life, its eyelids still weighted closed.

"My eyes! My eyes!" Tony cried, doing a superb impression of the menacing half-whisper of Peter Lorre. "They poured hot lead into my eyes. But I did not talk, Master… I swear! I did not talk!"

It broke the ice. Everybody howled with laughter as Tony shambled away, limping, back towards the bedroom. The tension that had been in the air after the incident with Frannie drained away. Alicia stepped unsteadily over to the low cabinet in the corner by the fireplace and put on a record. The buzz of conversation resumed.

Tommy walked over and spoke to Joe, who was just about to pour himself and Margaret another drink. He put a hand on Joe's arm and drew him to one side.

"I think we ought to go look for Frankie-boy," he said.

Joe shrugged.

"Aw, he'll come back," Joe said. He jerked a thumb towards the front door. "It's freezing out there."

Hearing them, Jerry unhooked his tenor from its cord and

went over to the closet by the door. He reached in, pulled out his overcoat and began shrugging into it. Joe saw him.

"Okay. All right," Joe said. "We'll take my car."

Tony returned from the bedroom, having put back the sheet he'd used and saw that the other guys were preparing to leave. Quickly realizing what was going on he went to get his own topcoat. Within moments, they were all muffled up and heading out the front door onto the dry, hard-packed snow.

Just as they were going out, Alicia put down her drink, went into the bedroom and came out wearing her coat. She was still uneasy on her feet and she went to the open door and stood there, holding onto it for support, looking after the retreating backs of the guys. Margaret came up behind her.

"Where ya going, Alicia?"

"To get some honey," Alicia said thickly, and stepped out into the cold night air.

Margaret looked at Tina and Francine, who were at her elbow, shrugged, and closed the door. Alicia was like that. She had this thing about honey when she got gassed. Somebody once told her, or maybe she read it somewhere, that honey was the best thing when you were getting too smashed. It was supposed to break down the alcohol in the system, by replacing the natural fruit-sugar in the blood that alcohol burned up at a greater rate than the body could produce it. Maybe it worked. Margaret had never tried it. But she'd think Alicia would think to bring her own honey with her in the first place. She always waited until she was almost legless, then went off in search, as if it were some magical cure.

The three girls walked back into the party room and stood around the fire, holding their hands out to the crackling flames, to take off the chill they had felt while standing by the door.

Outside, the guys started piling into Joe's new Lincoln Continental as he went around wiping the frost from the windows with a de-icer aerosol and a cloth. Jerry was about to follow Tommy and Tony into the car when he suddenly walked away a few paces and knelt down, examining the snow-covered ground. Tommy, who was still holding open the rear passenger door of the car, called out.

"What're you doing?"

"Checking for tracks," Jerry said, rising slowly to his feet,

"Oh, now we got a Tonto," Joe said, cackling at his own joke.

Tony said: "Ten bucks says Frannie's down at The Chalet, laughing over a beer. I'll bet that was one of those phony rubber bald heads."

Jerry returned to the car, then glanced back at a set of footprints in the snow that seemed to trail off towards the woods on the lower slopes.

"You have a flashlight, Joe?" he asked. He pointed to where he had just been kneeling. "I'm gonna take the jeep into the woods."

Alicia wandered up to the car and stood beside Jerry. She slowly bent down and gathered up a handful of snow which she put to her face like a mudpack. As Joe was rummaging around inside the car for a flashlight, Jerry noticed her beside him.

"You okay?" he said.

From behind the snow-mask, Alicia slowly, drunkenly, smiled.

"No."

"Why don't you take something?"

"I need some honey, that's all."

"Honey! How can you eat honey when you're feeling nauseous?"

Alicia dropped the snow and stared stupidly. "Come with me, Zippy," she slurred.

"I can't. You go into town with the guys and get some honey. I gotta look for Frannie."

He waved vaguely towards the woods. For a moment, Alicia

studied him, looking concerned. Then she climbed slowly into the back of the car.

"Here, Tonto," Joe called, holding out a flashlight through the open car window. Jerry took it. Joe started the engine and got ready to release the brake. Then he looked out at Jerry.

"I should let that pecker freeze to death," he said, his breath billowing out in miniature white clouds as he spoke. "I could be getting laid by now."

He cringed suddenly, realizing Alicia was in the rear seat.

"Excuse me, Alicia," he said quickly, embarrassed. But she did not seem to have heard.

Joe let out the handbrake and the tires crunched on the packed snow as the car moved slowly away. From the passenger seat, his window down, Tommy called out to Jerry.

"Jerry—you look for tracks. If we don't find him at The Chalet, we'll come back here and all fan out into the woods."

Jerry waved his agreement. As the lights of the car retreated, it became suddenly dark around the outside of the ski cottage. Jerry flicked on the flashlight and began to examine the snow for further tracks. Around the house itself, there were footprints and tire marks just about everywhere. But beyond where the Lincoln had been parked was the single set of prints snaking off into the darkness in the direction of the woods. Jerry walked over to his Bronco jeep, climbed in, started the engine and drove slowly away, leaning out the window, trying to follow the trail as he drove.

The full moon overhead picked out the dotted pines on the slopes as tall, dark blue cones, pointing up at the clear, cloudless sky. In the silver half-light, the large, rubber doll with staring eyes and wild hair, that Jerry kept as a mascot on the dashboard of his jeep, looked particularly ugly.

He steered the sturdy little vehicle carefully down between the trees, which gradually became more dense as he entered the woods. Occasionally, branches stretched out in his path, brushing across the radiator and windshield, depositing their powdery coats of snow in clouds. On one branch ahead, Jerry spotted what seemed like a peculiar, out-of-place shadow. He drove forward until the branch touched the front of the hood, then stopped the jeep and got out. Stepping into the glare of the headlights, he reached up and grasped the branch and something fell to the snow at his feet. He bent down and picked it up. It was the wig that Frannie had been wearing at the party.

His hand inside the crown, he held it up, turning it around, studying it carefully, in the beam of the flashlight. Then he stuffed it into the pocket of his baggy, tan chinos and moved on, on foot.

As they waited for the guys to return, the three girls stood around the fire back at the ski house, discussing the evening's events. The main lights were still switched off and the flickering firelight threw their distorted, dancing shadows grotesquely over the walls.

"You think it was a joke?" Margaret was saying to Francine. "I almost shit!"

"Coming from Tony it would have been funny," Francine said. "But...it looked so real."

"Yeah," Tina said. "It didn't have stubbles like he shaved it. And did you see his eyes?"

Margaret stood up from her crouching position by the fire and looked over at the large picture window in the opposite wall. She could faintly see the snowy slopes, tinged by silver moonlight and the shapes of the pines huddled vaguely on the skyline in the distance. She shuddered involuntarily.

"Cut it out, Tina," she said. "Now you're giving me the willies. I wish they'd come back."

She rubbed her arms and was not surprised to discover that, despite the warmth of the fire, she had broken out in goosebumps.

There was a muffled noise from outside. They all heard it.

"That must be them," Tina said, as their three heads wheeled to look toward the entrance foyer. Tina walked off toward the front door. The small entrance hall was in darkness. She opened the door.

Before she could move or cry out, two hands reached out and grabbed her under the arms, lifting her off her feet. She gasped and began drumming her fists on the shoulders of her assailant, then gasped again with a choking cry when she saw that it was Frannie, holding her, carrying her backwards into the house. His head was still completely, ridiculously bald. Then she saw his eyes.

They were wide and staring, the pupils dilated enormously into round, jet black discs, blotting out all the color from the irises. Only a trace of the whites of his eyes showed slightly around the edges of those horrible, fathomless, black pits, giving him the look of an alien, only partly-human, eerie and other-worldly.

Realizing for sure that this was definitely not some kind of joke, Tina shrieked, drumming her fists and kicking. Then she was hurled backwards into the fireplace, feeling the flames immediately searing up the backs of her legs and her body and, as she threw back her arms to save herself, felt her hands and forearms painfully scorched. And she smelt her own flesh burning as she writhed and twisted and screamed in agony, trying to get up out of the fire.

Paralyzed with horror for a second at what they saw, the other two girls suddenly and simultaneously came to their senses and tried to grab Frannie as he crouched over Tina, holding her down in the fireplace. He wheeled around as he felt their hands upon him and, with a snarl, punched Margaret savagely in the stomach. And as she doubled up, retching, he followed through with a fierce, rapid punch in her mouth. Then, reaching down, he seized a poker from the fireplace and swung it mercilessly at Francine, catching her a terrible blow to the side of the head.

Tina, still screeching deafeningly and horribly, fell forward out of the fire onto the rug. By now she was a living flame, her hair a terrible, crackling halo, her clothes a hellish series of wreaths of fire. Her tortured cries rang out in the night as she writhed and twitched in sheer agony at Frannie's feet.

It turned out to be one hell of a party, all right.

CHAPTER 5

JERRY HEARD Tina's nightmarish screams echoing out in the valley through the woods. He realized the sound came from the direction of the ski house and ran back to the jeep. He jumped in, switched on the ignition and rammed it into four-wheel drive, yanking on the wheel as he let out the clutch, steering the vehicle in a wide U-turn, around between trees.

Even the heavy-duty tires on the jeep could not hold perfectly on the packed snow at speed and the Bronco skidded wildly, swinging from side to side as Jerry aimed it up the uneven slope toward the house. He skidded to a halt outside the front door, cut the engine, leapt out and ran inside.

Peering ahead as he entered the foyer, Jerry almost retched as a horrible, totally unfamiliar smell, a stench of something raw and burning, was wafted to his nostrils. Warily, he moved forward, keeping close to the wall as he approached the open doorway into the room where the party had been. He could hear nothing. The flickering flames from the fire threw dancing yellow lights around the walls. From where he stood, just outside the doorway of the room, he could see the table lamp that Tony had used as a spotlight, still switched on, but lying on its side on the floor. Then he began to notice other tell-tale signs of a violent struggle—chairs upended, a coffee table on its side, a bottle and some glasses smashed beneath the drinks table. He edged forward and peered into the room. The strange, nauseating smell, like burning pork, grew stronger in his nostrils.

Then he looked towards the fireplace. There in an indistinguishable huddle, was what remained of the three girls, piled in the hearth, like some unsavory remnants of a charnel house. Flames still licked around the torsos that lay there in the wide fireplace among the embers. An arm stuck out in front, part of what looked like a charred face was visible near the top of the twisted heap of human flesh. And the stench, which he now recognized to his horror, was unbearable and made him gag into his hand.

"My God!" he gasped and instinctively hurried forward, trying to kick or stomp at the flames with his snow-soaked boots. Then he grabbed a pillow from the sofa along the side of the room and began beating at the flames licking up from the jumble of charred and smoldering bodies, causing clouds of woodsmoke to billow out into the room.

"Okay, okay, girls," Jerry panted, hardly realizing what he was doing or saying. "It's…gonna be all right…. Don't worry!"

Margaret's body, which had been on top of the pile, tumbled out, still burning. Frantically, Jerry looked around the room and spotted the full-length curtains which covered the sliding doors leading out onto the verandah. He ran over and swung upon them until a section snapped loose from the runners, and a large segment of curtain billowed down. But to Jerry's utter shock there, standing behind the place where the curtain had hung, was Frannie, looking like something out of a nightmare.

In the dim light, Frannie's bald head seemed almost pure white, like the skin of a corpse. His eyes bulged out of his head. He looked like he had gone stark raving mad.

Before Jerry could move, in the split instant that he was taking it all in, Frannie's hands shot out and clamped around his throat.

"No… Frannie! Take it easy…hey!" Jerry gasped, half-choking. At the same time he clawed frantically at Frannie's hands, trying to break the vice-like grip.

"Frannie...what happened? Let go a-me!" Jerry choked. "Can't you see they're burning in there!"

Realizing he could not break Frannie's tightening, steel grip, Jerry hurled all his weight sideways, grasping Frannie around the chest at the same time. It threw them both off balance and drew Frannie away from the terrace doors. Staggering, the pair lurched, locked together, through the main room of the cabin to the still-open front door. For a second they stood poised, grappling, Jerry's breath now coming in strangulated gasps as his windpipe was constricted more and more. He knew that at any moment now he would black out. His tongue was beginning to sag from his lolling lips and his eyes felt like they were bursting out of their sockets. Then, they toppled over, down the wooden steps at the front of the ski house and onto the snow outside.

The fall did it. Frannie, in an effort to save himself, released his grasp and, as they rolled over and over on the ground, Jerry managed to get to his feet quickly and stagger away, but Frannie was not far behind him. Jerry zigzagged, half stumbling and slipping on the snow as he ran. Frannie's frightening figure plodded along after him doggedly, his hands reaching out before him like a sleepwalker.

Pausing, Jerry bent down and grabbed a handful of snow, packed it into a tight ball and hurled it at Frannie's face. It was dead on target, but Frannie did not even blink as the snowball smashed itself into his cheek and shattered. He simply kept coming.

Jerry spotted the lights of a car coming up the hill on the road that skirted the plot where the ski house lay. He ran toward the road, waving his arms frantically, trying to flag down some assistance, but the car kept going, whooshing by into the night. Jerry wheeled and Frannie was almost on top of him.

"Frannie!" he gasped, hysterical with fear. "Leave me alone!"

Desperately, he swung a punch at Frannie's jaw with all his might. It connected and he felt his knuckles stinging with the impact. But the blow appeared to have no effect at all on the zombie-like, hairless, staring figure before him.

Frannie reached out, snarling, and grabbed Jerry simultaneously by the neck and by the crotch of his pants, lifted him bodily over his head and flung him into the branches of a nearby bush. Although the twigs and thorns scratched him, the wet snow that cascaded down from the upper reaches of the bush on his impact, acted like a cold, refreshing, sudden shower. Quickly regaining his wind, Jerry scrambled down on the opposite side of the bush and charged away. But Frannie was still following.

They were cutting back towards the harrow public road that ran up from the town below, scything across the district of Hillsdale and on to an upstate intersection. And just at that time, hauling up the road at a steady speed, its huge headlights stabbing out into the night, came a heavy truck hauling a long, articulated trailer. The two men in the cab had bought some cans of beer and sandwiches on a stop-off a few miles back and were tucking into their snack as they continued their haul, with the radio turned on full blast.

As he took a long pull on his beer, Ralphie, the relief driver in the passenger seat, saw something out of the corner of his eye on the road about a hundred yards ahead. He lowered his drink and peered forward, squinting through the glare of the headlights as they ate up the road. There was something...

"Hey, Pete, watch out!" he shouted.

Just as he shouted, he grabbed the wheel and yanked on it. But Pete, the driver, had also caught sight of some moving shapes on the periphery of the headlights' high-beam range. He tugged the wheel the other way instinctively, over-correcting, and the long trailer began to jackknife on the icy road.

Up ahead, only a few yards away now, Frannie was momentarily blinded by the glare of the truck's lights and it gave Jerry the chance he needed. With all his might he pushed the white-faced zombie away from him. Right into the path of the oncoming truck. Jerry dived for the snowbank by the side of the road.

Frozen in the headlights' beams, Frannie threw up his arms to shield his weird, huge, black eyes from the glare. Then, when the truck was only inches away, he lunged out insanely with his fist in one maniacal, almost superhuman act of defiance, as if trying to punch the vehicle off the road. Then the tremendous impact of the huge chrome bumper bar stove in his ribs and dashed him to the asphalt.

Jerry lay face down in the snow, breathless. He raised his head, the powdery flakes clinging to his eyebrows and chin and the sides of his head. He stared towards the road to see the bulky, lifeless form of Frannie lying there. Suddenly, he remembered the girls back at the house, scrambled to his feet and dashed off in that direction.

By this time, the huge truck had skidded to a halt, sitting askew across the road. As the two men jumped down from the cab, Pete spotted the running figure of Jerry heading for the ski house which was just discernible as a black shape against the snow on the right-hand side of the road.

"Hey you!" Pete yelled. "Come back here!"

But Jerry kept on running toward the house. Pete joined Ralphie, kneeling by the still form of Frannie on the road. Pete took his wrist to feel for a pulse. But before he had time to do so, Frannie suddenly, convulsively, struggled quickly to his feet, reeled around in a few staggering steps, then fell backwards into the snow at the roadside. Pete ran over and laid his ear against Frannie's chest, listening. After a moment, he looked up, grim-faced.

"Ralphie-boy," he said. "He's a goner." Ralphie nodded toward the ski house.

"I'm going after that son of a bitch!" he said angrily. He went over to the truck, leaned into the cab for a moment to take a pistol from the glove compartment. Releasing the safety catch, he hefted it in his hand and headed off up the slope toward the house.

Inside Jerry was sobbing like a child. He was kneeling on the pinewood floor, his face in his hands, the remains of three girls' charred bodies arranged in a row before the fireplace. He had pulled the smoldering, blackened torsos out of the fire and laid them out on the rug. Suffering from severe shock, Jerry barely realized what he was seeing or doing. Then a voice rasped out behind him.

"Hold it!" the voice spat. "Move and you're dead!"

From the shadows by the door, the truck driver stepped cautiously forward, aiming a .38 caliber revolver at Jerry's head.

Jerry continued to sob fitfully, his shoulders shaking, almost as if the man had not been there.

Ralphie moved in closer and gazed for a moment uncomprehendingly at the three unfamiliar shapes in the dying firelight. Then it dawned on him what he was seeing. And he had to turn his face away.

"Jesus Christ!" he said.

His hands had begun to tremble and he had to use both of them to steady the gun as he held it out before him, still pointing it at Jerry.

"Don't you move!" he said in a trembling voice as he turned back to Jerry.

Still stunned and shattered by his horrific experience, Jerry looked slowly up at the stranger standing over him, then down at what was left of the girls. Like a needle of light darting into his brain, he suddenly realized the predicament he was in. This man, this tall stranger with the gun, thought he was to blame for all the carnage. He turned again to look at the man and spread his hands wide, pleadingly.

"I'll blow your fuckin' brains out if you move!" the man

rasped, more certain of himself now. Then he called back over his shoulder, towards the open door. "Pete! Get some cops down here fast!"

There was a muffled, answering yell and as Jerry's eyes darted quickly around the room, taking in the situation, he heard a cab door slam and the sound of the truck pulling away. He looked up at the man again, pleading with his eyes.

"I...I didn't do this," Jerry said.

"Bullshit you didn't!" the man spat. He was nervous as hell. "Just don't move. I'll shoot." The gun, aimed at Jerry's face, was trembling visibly in the man's grip. As the trucker spoke, Jerry slowly, imperceptibly moved his left hand, furthest from the man and out of his line of vision. He felt around the floor, searching.

"Just try something...go ahead," the man said.

Sweat beaded out on his forehead.

Jerry, who was still looking up at the man, holding his gaze, felt his hand come into contact with an object. It was warm, hard, metallic. The poker from the fireplace. Carefully, he eased his fingers around it tightly. Then, ducking to one side like lightning, he swung the iron and hurled it at the man's head. As the truck-driver instinctively flinched to dodge the flying object, Jerry leapt to his feet and darted by him, out through the foyer and the open front door.

"Don't!" he heard the man screaming behind him as he ran. "I'll shoot you. I'll shoot!"

Jerry reached the parked jeep as the man appeared in the doorway, squeezing off shots at random, still with both hands on the gun. He dived into the driver's seat and felt a sharp stabbing pain, like a blow, jab his right shoulder. The bullet came out the other side and smashed open the face of the ugly rubber mascot doll on the dashboard.

As he gunned the engine, fighting back the searing pain in his shoulder, a pain that was red hot and icy cold at the same time, Jerry could hear the man's voice rasping out:

"I told ya, I told ya!"

And more shots rang out and as the jeep pulled away, wheels skidding on the snow, another bullet smashed through the windshield.

Ralph stood on the steps of the ski house, still squeezing the trigger, even though he had emptied the .38. His face was a mask of loathing and uncontrollable anger.

The bouncing of the jeep on the uneven terrain made the pain in Jerry's shoulder throb agonizingly, but he kept his foot down on the gas pedal. At the western extremity of the ski house property, he drove straight through a low wooden fence and headed into the dark safety of the trees beyond.

CHAPTER 6

Lieutenant Dennis Jennings used the headlights of the parked ambulance to see by as he jotted down notes in his little red book. He glanced up at the extremely attractive girl standing before him as he leaned on the door of his dark blue Chevrolet Monte Carlo. She was staring past him to where the ambulance attendants were lifting shapeless things under sheets into the open rear doors of their vehicle. Those...things...she was thinking, were all that was left of her friends, Margaret, Tina and Francine. Only the body of Frannie had been recognizable as such, had borne the outline of a human figure under its white coverlet. Beyond the ambulance, on the wooden steps outside the ski house, Tony, Joe and Tommy were sitting huddled together, not speaking, not looking at each other; just staring out into the night expressionlessly. Nobody even seemed to feel the cold anymore.

"How long have you known Zipkin?" the Lieutenant asked.

Alicia sniffled and dabbed at her eyes with a paper tissue.

"I met Jerry last summer." There was no emotion in her voice.

"Do you live together?"

"No... we..." She flashed an angry look at him with those large, violet-blue eyes. "I don't have to answer your questions,"

44

she said angrily. She started to move away, but Lieutenant Jennings grasped her firmly by the arm. She winced and shook herself free, but made no further sign of moving.

"Yes you do. You know, Miss…"

He glanced down swiftly at his notepad.

"Sweeny," he finished. "You're lucky you're alive. Your boyfriend could just have easily turned loose on you."

Alicia shook her head, her mouth tight and determined.

"Zippy…uh…Jerry didn't do this," she said.

"Look, Miss Sweeny," the Lieutenant said. "What's your first name?"

She didn't answer but looked down at her clasped hands. Lieutenant Jennings glanced at his notebook again.

"Alicia," he said. "I have a daughter your age. She's coming up from the city to go skiing with me tomorrow. I'd much rather do that than chase after a murderer. But she could just as easily have been one of those girls in there."

He inclined his head toward the cottage where the three young men he'd interviewed earlier were sitting silently.

"I'll talk to my attorney before I talk to you," Alicia said.

Jennings shook his head slowly and exhaled through his clenched teeth.

"Damned television shows!" he murmured to himself as he turned away.

Jerry didn't know how long, nor how far he had been driving before he came to the service station. The pain in his shoulder was getting worse, much worse, and it was difficult to think straight. All he knew was that he had been heading south, back toward the city. For what seemed like miles, he'd painfully wrenched the wheel of the jeep back and forth, negotiating the trees in the dark woods, at the same time being tossed around in his driver's seat by the unevenness of the land. At last he'd made it up a slip road that doubled back and appeared to be heading toward the freeway intersection that would put him on the route leading back to town.

It was then that he'd seen the all-night station. There was a lighted phone booth at the far end of the low service buildings. He wheeled the jeep into the forecourt, then around the side and parked facing the road. He cut the lights and got out. Keeping his right hand in his pocket so that he would disturb the wounded shoulder as little as possible, he fumbled around with the icy, near-frozen fingers of his left hand, trying to find some change. Eventually he located the coins and went into the phone booth and dropped them into the slot. As he was doing so the sprung door of the booth swung shut against his wounded shoulder and a searing pain lanced all down his right arm, making him wince. For a moment, he leaned on the opposite glass panel of the booth, eyes watering, waiting for the spasm to subside. Then at last, he managed to dig out his wallet and, still using only one hand, fumbled out the white printed business card with the name and telephone number on it. He dialed, with the phone wedged between his left ear and left shoulder.

As he stood listening to the purr of the ringing tone at the other end, a police patrol car swung off the road and into the service station forecourt. While the attendant pumped gas into the tank, the two uniformed policemen got out and stood chatting.

A women's voice answered at the other end. "Hello," Jerry said. "Dr. Blume, please."

He kept his eyes on the two cops as he spoke. There in the lighted booth, he was in plain view of them both. But neither glanced his way. They stomped their boots against the cold, their hands thrust deep in their pockets while the attendant went off to get some change.

"It's personal," Jerry said into the phone. "Jerry Zipkin."

There was a pause, then a click, then a fresh voice, a man's voice, spoke.

"Davie?" Jerry said. He winced as yet another dart of pain shot through his shoulder.

"Fine…real good," he said. "Listen, Dave, I mean Doc…I have a little problem. I've been shot. What? No, no. No big deal…a…a hunter. You know, one of those once-a-year guys. Upstate near Hillsdale. Well, I don't want some stranger digging away on me and you have all my records. It would only take me…uh…an hour, hour and a half, maybe, to get there."

One of the two patrolmen glanced over toward the phone booth. He stared briefly, then said something to his partner.

"First floor, emergency room?" Jerry said, still eyeing the cops. "Uh, Dave, what about your office? Don't I rate private treatment?"

The patrolman was strolling slowly over towards the booth. The perspiration broke out on Jerry's brow.

"Yeah…good. Uh, thanks, Davie," he said hurriedly and hung up the receiver. Without looking at the police officer, who was about ten yards away, Jerry walked briskly towards his jeep, climbed in and started the engine.

"Hey, fella!" the patrolman called. But Jerry revved his engine, crammed the stick shift into gear and began to roll forward.

The cop turned and started running back toward his partner and their cruiser. But halfway there he hit an icy patch on the asphalt and both feet shot out forward from under him. As he gunned the engine and turned to pull back onto the road, Jerry looked in his rear-view mirror just in time to see the cop doing an extremely ungraceful and very painful backwards fall, his arms clawing the air, his feet pumping like he was trying to run but getting nowhere. The poor guy was bound to land on the base of his spine. It had to be an ambulance job. Nasty, but lucky for Jerry.

On the highway back to town, Jerry tried to live up to his nickname, without attracting the attention of any more cops.

CHAPTER 7

THE RECEPTIONIST on the fifth floor of the Metropolitan Hospital was pretty nifty. She was both, in fact, pretty and nifty. She seemed able to do two things at once. While she was listening to Jerry telling her he had an appointment to see Dr. Blume, she kept on reading her current copy of *Cosmopolitan*. She kept reading, even when she picked up the handset from the switch panel on the white-topped, kidney-shaped desk and dialed. She still didn't look up when someone answered at the other end and she said:

"Mr. Zipkin's here to see you. Says you're expecting him."

She even got Jerry's name right, too, without making any unfunny cracks about Zipcodes and Zip Goes A-Million and things like that. If his shoulder hadn't felt like it was on fire and generating inter-muscular lightning, Jerry might even have tried to engage her in conversation. As it was, it was all he could do to keep from screwing his face into a permanent grimace and biting on his tongue. With his left hand, he held on to the edge of the desk for support.

At last, the receptionist actually looked up. She replaced the handset and, fluttering her long, dark lashes coyly, said:

"Okay, Mr. Zipkin. You can wait for the doctor in his office."

She wondered if he'd got a good enough squint at her ample

boobs while she'd been eyes-down, look-in. They usually did. That's why she always pretended to read. It saved all the nervous eye darting and peculiar facial expressions that she usually got if she looked directly at the male visitors. She sat up straight, throwing back her shoulders and making her breasts stick out even more prominently against the material of her uniform, as she pointed with her left hand.

"Straight down the hall..." Jerry managed a smile.

"I know," he said, and moved off, his right hand still thrust into the pocket of his chinos.

Dr. David Blume's office was tidily kept and furnished with a long, low, modern desk and a tubular-framed, straight-back chair facing it. The doctor's chair was a swivel affair with winged arms. Along the wall opposite the desk was a four-seater leather couch. Jerry chose the couch.

As he sat there, he glanced idly across at the numerous framed diplomas on the wall behind the desk. The fine print and script lettering was too small to read from across the room, but he could discern the large lettered headings of each one:

Metropolitan Hospital—Surgery.

Down State Medical School.

Association of Orthopedic Surgery.

The fourth was an ordinary, standard college graduation diploma: Syracuse University, 1967.

"Zipkin. How the hell did you get yourself shot?"

Jerry wheeled and Dr. Blume was standing framed in the doorway. Jerry hadn't heard it open. He stood up.

"Hey, David...how you doing?" he said.

Dr. Blume reached out and grasped Jerry's right hand and shook it. Jerry winced with the pain that shot through his shoulder.

"Hey, let me see that," Dr. Blume said, noticing the dark brown bloodstains on Jerry's coat sleeve. He peered closely at the torn material, back and front, two small round holes that could have been cigarette burns.

"Go into that room," he said. "Take off your coat." Jerry went into the examining room, a small anteroom off the main office. Dr. Blume came in and washed his hands at a basin in the corner. Painfully, Jerry struggled out of his coat, then lay down on a low examination table that was covered by a fresh white disposable paper sheet. Dr. Blume came over and, cutting away part of Jerry's shabby Banion shirt with a pair of scissors, began to inspect and clean up the wound. As he went to work on it, dabbing away with cotton swabs and applying antiseptic from a small bottle, he kept glancing curiously at Jerry's face.

"You look terrible," he said at last. "Is this what it takes to get to see you?"

Jerry nodded, noncommittally.

"It passed right through," Dr. Blume said. "Pretty clean. Did you get the guy's name?"

"No."

"I have to fill out a report," Dr. Blume said, cleaning out the wound. "It's too bad you didn't get his name. These guys will shoot at anything that moves."

The doctor didn't notice, but Jerry's eyes suddenly filled with panic. Yet he managed to keep it out of his voice when he spoke next.

"Hey...what report?" he said, as if they were talking about filling in a Society Security form. "It was an accident. Why get the poor guy in trouble?"

Dr. Blume sighed.

"The rules, Jerry. We have to report all gunshot and knife wounds. Now, tell me what happened."

The doctor was just finishing off dressing and bandaging Jerry's shoulder.

"I told you," Jerry said.

Dr. Blume took a small pencil-type flashlight from the pocket of his white coat and leaned over Jerry, peering into his eyes.

"Try not to blink," he said.

Jerry stared back into the doctor's eyes as the tiny beam probed into his own. He couldn't help thinking of Frannie's strange, black, staring eyes.

"Are you sure it was a hunter?"

"Yeah," Jerry said. "I didn't see him, but—"

"Why don't you want me to report it?"

"It was an accident," Jerry said emphatically. "I don't want to make it a big deal."

Blume moved away, signaling that it was all right for Jerry to get up off the examining couch. Jerry followed him out of the anteroom into the office and over to the desk. He stood by while the doctor filled in a prescription form. As Blume leaned over the paper on which he was writing, Jerry noticed something on a sheet of white paper just in front of the Doctor's hands. He reached down and picked it up. It was several strands of hair. The doc's hair. He looked at Blume's receding hairline.

"Fill this prescription," Blume said, looking up and proffering the small printed form. "Antibiotics. You should really rest, too." Jerry held up the lock of hair.

"Hey, Davie," he said, "you going bald already?"

Blume glanced at the hair, then looked down at his hands embarrassedly, searching for something to say. Then he ran a hand nervously through his hair. He still did not answer. Reaching in his desk drawer, he brought out a little polystyrene phial of pills, tipped two out into his palm and popped them into his mouth and swallowed them.

"You sick?" Jerry said, frowning curiously.

"Aspirins," Dr. Blume said. "The job has a lot of pressures they don't tell you about in med school." He glanced up at Jerry. "But I don't fool around with anything stronger than these anymore—you know that."

He placed the pills back in his desk drawer. Jerry looked at the prescription he had taken from the doctor.

"Just like that," he said. "Instant drugs. It's kind of a shame you don't fool around with anything anymore. What convenience you could have had."

Dr. Blume smirked boyishly.

"The risk was half the fun," he said with a wink.

Jerry struggled into his coat, leaving the right sleeve dangling, empty. He was about to turn and leave, then remembered.

"Uh, what do I owe you?

Dr. Blume smiled and waved the question aside. "Forget it. What is a bullet-wound dressing between old friends?

Jerry nodded gratefully and went to the door. With his hand on the handle, he turned around.

"Well, Davie," he said, "I'll see you the next time I get shot."

Blume smiled weakly. And Jerry went out. Jerry didn't see it, but the expression on Dr. Blume's face as soon as he was out of the room, was no longer a smile. It was that of a very harassed and worried man.

CHAPTER 8

WENDY FLEMMING HAD HAD to confide in somebody. And when you're twenty-nine, divorced, living alone on low alimony in the Bronx and have what can hardly be described as a full social life, you don't have a lot of choice when you want to tell somebody that you're worried because your hair keeps falling out. So it had to be Stephanie, Mrs. Stephanie Andretti, the neighbor across the hall with the two cute kids.

At one point, Wendy had thought of phoning Edward, asking him to meet her. But then, she reasoned, what could she say? Gee, Eddie-baby, I know you're a busy man, running for Congress and all that but, like, d'you think you could spare me some time 'cause…well, uh, my goddamn hair's falling out and I keep having these nightmares and headaches? I mean, I'm not trying to start anything up all over again or anything like that and I know we agreed not to bother each other, but…well, I just didn't have anyone else I could turn to.

Worse still, what would he say? She could just imagine his reaction. He'd think: Huh! So the little bitch is trying to muscle in again, now that I'm doing pretty well and am almost a sure thing for Congress. What is this, some kind of a shakedown? Hair falling out? Jesus, I've heard some lines in my time but that just about takes the Academy Award for Limp Excuses. Why can't she go see a headshrinker like everybody else in this crazy goddamn town, the neurotic little bitch?

So she dismissed that one fairly quickly. Then she'd started thinking about her old friends, the ones from college and she began to realize what her marriage to Eddie had done in that line. The simple fact was that, during her life with Edward, she'd simply lost touch. For a long time before and after their marriage, she and Eddie had had time only for themselves and when the whole wild, lovely, heady, screwy kaboodle had fallen apart at the seams and lay in tatters on the divorce lawyer's office floor, it was too late to start creeping back, phoning people and saying? Hi, how are ya? Remember me? We used to be friends at college, Class of '67.

Besides, they'd probably all moved apartments, jobs, or cities, even. They'd be married, maybe, raising kids out in California and stuff like that. Some of them might even be dead.

And it seemed like every direction she turned, she was in a cul-de-sac. A plain, grey, concrete, boring Kafkaesque nightmare wall shut her in on all sides. Just like the walls of her apartment. No friends, only acquaintances, and that only through being scrunched up in a little living-unit box in a thirty-story high rise for human battery-hens. Alone, with her TV and her broken and tarnished, thoroughly loused-up past.

So it had had to be Stephanie—Mrs. Andretti from across the hall.

In her black silk slip and bra, Wendy stooped over the kitchen sink with the suds running down the sides of her face, behind her ears, uncomfortable rivulets escaping down areas of her neck. Some of the shampoo even found its way into her eyes, like it always did, no matter how tightly she shut them.

Stephanie stood behind her, leaning over her, gently massaging the liquid shampoo into Wendy's scalp. There was, at least, something soothing about having your head massaged like that. In the background, from the living room, despite the soap in her ears, Wendy could hear the sound of the television, as Jason and Samantha sat watching the late afternoon kids' programs.

"You *sure* you didn't use any coloring?" Stephanie said as her fingers gently worked the shampoo into the roots of Wendy's hair. She noticed as she worked away one or two small patches of skin where no hair appeared to be growing at all. Wendy had cut her hair short and restyled it slightly, in hope that it would grow naturally again.

"I'm sure," Wendy said thickly, trying to speak without getting suds in her mouth. "Jesus Christ, Stephanie, why would I want to do anything to impair my natural beauty?"

Mrs. Andretti noted the weary sarcasm in Wendy's voice. She sighed. That worn, hard veneer that life eventually seemed to bestow upon most people at some stage, had come early to Wendy.

"Well, I just thought maybe you saw some grey hairs or something," Stephanie said.

"At my tender age?" Wendy said and the tired off-handedness was there again in her voice. "Maybe when I get as old as you…"

Stephanie was herself only approaching forty. So she placed a hand on the back of Wendy's head and pushed forwards and down so that her face went into the water in the sink basin. Wendy came up spluttering and laughing at the same time.

"Just kidding, just kidding," she gurgled.

"Anyway," Stephanie said, as Wendy reached for the towel to wipe the soap from her eyes, "the haircut removed any damaged hair."

She picked up a plastic bottle containing a clear yellow liquid. Flicking open the top, she guided Wendy back to the sink again, made her lean over and squirted the liquid liberally all over her hair.

"This will do the trick," Stephanie said. "It has animal protein in it."

"Yeccchhh!" Wendy grimaced, still leaning over the sink.

"Well, what do you think your hair is made of?" Stephanie said dryly.

Wendy didn't say anything. It was just the word "animal" that for her conjured up fat and bones and raw tissue and all kinds of unsavory ingredients. She wondered if any particular type of animal was slaughtered—just so that women could put proteins in their hair.

"How often do you wash it?" Stephanie asked, "Sometimes too much washing can make your hair fall out."

Wendy tried to remember. But while she was thinking, another idea occurred to Stephanie. She stopped rubbing in the protein and smiled to herself.

"Wendy, when was the last time you had any?" she said, wickedly.

In all innocence, Wendy straightened up, squinting through the soapsuds and said: "Any what?"

"You know," Stephanie said, winking.

"You writing a column?" Wendy said with an indignant smirk.

"Sometimes *that* can make your hair fall out," Stephanie said, with the air of having delivered a great revelation.

Wendy turned around, pulled the plug out of the sink basin and reached for a towel. As she began to dab her hair dry gently, she said:

"Stephanie, I just don't believe you sometimes. Just because you're a horny, divorced nymphomaniac who pulls out her hair when she's not getting her cavity filled..."

"I'm not making it up," Stephanie said, emphatically. "I read it in *Cosmo*. It affects your biorhythms."

The sink emptied with a loud, prolonged gurgling sound, almost a note of disapproval, like someone with a bad stomach. Wendy continued to dry her hair ever so carefully.

Just then, little Samantha wandered into the room carrying a cup, half-filled with a grey-colored liquid, a mixture of water and paint. She had been knocking off a couple of impressionistic watercolors while watching television. Or maybe they were abstracts. From the amount of paint down her bib-fronted playsuit, she might even have been experimenting in some form of action-painting, too. More likely, though, her brother Jason had probably decided to paint her. She held out the cup to Wendy.

"Fill this up, please," she said, all businesslike, with the air of a Michelangelo ordering a few more gallons of high-sheen gloss for the Pontiff's bathroom ceiling.

Wendy took the cup, turned on the tap and rinsed it out. As the paint washed away she realized it was not emptying down the drain properly with the water. She reached into the plughole and felt around. Her fingers came up with a huge mass of sodden hair. Her own hair. It looked even more horrible with the sickly greenish paint streaks in it.

"Stephanie!" she gasped, turning pale and looking quite frightened, holding up the lump of dripping hair.

Stephanie's eyes widened as she saw the amount of hair that Wendy was grasping. Then, seeing that Samantha was still waiting for the fresh water, she took the cup from Wendy and filled it, handing it back to her daughter.

"Here, Samantha," she said quickly. "Why don't you take your brother home and watch TV there. I don't want you spilling paint on Wendy's carpet."

Obediently, Samantha nodded and went into the living room to collect her brother. Stephanie watched her go out, then turned to see Wendy standing with both fists to her temples, her whitened knuckles kneading into the sides of her head, her face creased up as if she were in intense pain.

After a moment, Wendy took a deep, deep breath, then exhaled slowly, lowering her hands. The tension went out of her body and her forehead and face muscles relaxed. She blew out, as if relieved. She looked earnestly at Stephanie.

"Stephanie," she said quietly, "something's wrong with me. I…I've been having these awful nightmares. I haven't had a decent night's sleep in I don't know how long, and these headaches are driving me up the walls."

She went over to the kitchen counter, picked up a pack of cigarettes, took one out and lit it. She closed her eyes, inhaling deeply, feeling the smoke harsh against the back of her throat. Her lungs felt tight and constricted. She blew out the smoke through her nostrils, coughing a little. Stephanie simply stood there, watching her with concern.

Wendy looked at her bashfully, as if about to make a confession, and said: "Guess what this weekend is."

Stephanie shrugged. Her deep amber eyes were still tracking over Wendy's drawn features.

"What is this weekend?"

"It'll be a year since Eddie and I broke up." Stephanie sighed and nodded knowingly. "So? That's what's wrong?"

Wendy lowered her eyes. Stephanie stepped up to her and placed her hands on Wendy's shoulders.

"Babycakes," she said, "take it from a veteran. Nothing affected me more than when the Beatles broke up. My divorce was nothing compared to that. I felt betrayed. Then I realized that they had become a part of the past. That's all. Part of the past. And we live now."

Wendy looked at her, disbelievingly. What in hell was Stephanie talking about? What had the Beatles got to do with—?

"Don't you see?" Stephanie went on, looking directly into her eyes. "We're in the future and the Beatles are in the past. They should be jealous of us! I'll bet they are."

Wendy was thinking: she doesn't know. It's not just the past or anything like that. There's something else. But how can she know, when even I don't know?

Then she thought: Jesus Christ, what's happening to me?

But, just for Stephanie's benefit more than for anything else, Wendy said:

"How can I forget Eddie when his gorgeous puss is plastered all over the city?"

And Stephanie said: "I didn't say forget him. But the Eddie you know is part of the past, like the Beatles…"

CHAPTER 9

ACTUALLY, Eddie's puss wasn't anything like gorgeous when Jerry Zipkin saw it. It was hideous. It was death-white, like a morgue mugshot. There were no pupils or irises in the eyes: they were empty, blank, pure white. It gave the face a bizarre and frightening stare, like a zombie. Almost the way Frannie had looked, the night he attacked Jerry and the girls. The only difference was, Flemming's eyes were white, not black. And he wasn't completely bald. Only half-bald. One half of his head—the left side—was perfectly normal, with the neat, distinctive haircut that Flemming normally sported, the one that TV viewers all over New York had seen a thousand times. The other side was as bald as a bowling ball.

Then, as Jerry stared, the hydraulically operated doors of the subway car closed with a hiss and the

bizarre, half-bald, empty-eyed, corpse-white face of Edward Flemming was blocked from view. The car door windows were covered with aerosol-spray graffiti, the work of vandals. Maybe even the same vandals who, with a few deft squirts of white paint, had defaced the subway poster of Edward Flemming and turned him from a handsome, debonair young politician into a nightmarish, half-human monster. Just before the doors were completely closed, Jerry caught sight of the slogan beneath the defaced poster. It said:

HERE IS THE FUTURE — EDWARD FLEMMING FOR CONGRESS.

Those vandals hadn't known how close they came to the truth when they'd gone to work on Edward Flemming's picture. The kind of human parody that they'd made of him was, in a way, part of the future. The vandals didn't know it. Nor did the guys who dreamed up Flemming's campaign slogan. Nor did Jerry Zipkin. But soon, Jerry was going to find out about that future.

Jerry crouched in one of the side seats that ran lengthways along the subway car as it pulled out of the station, somewhere on the West Side of Manhattan. He was exhausted and badly needed to rest up somewhere and it showed in his pale, wasted face. But he could not afford to hole up. Not now. Not with three dead girls and a dead man lying in the cold storage drawers of a morgue in the Berkshire area of upstate New York, and the boys from Homicide all looking for him. They'd be out there even now, checking out his last few addresses, looking for friends who might know where he'd been hiding out. No, he couldn't take the chance. It had had to be the jeep, curled up in the back, trying to catch some sleep in the chill February night, hoping that a patrolman wouldn't come along and find him parked on a vacant lot out in the slum quarters.

He wondered if they'd put a bug on Alicia's phone. She was the only one he could trust; the only person he'd dared to risk calling. Even if they didn't tap her phone and heard him arrange to meet her—using a disguised voice and a phony name, of course—they could still get to him. They could put a tail on her, twenty-four hours a day, follow her everywhere. And if they did, sooner or later she'd lead them to him. He didn't have much time. They were bound to catch up with him. So he had to work fast and try to figure things out, to somehow dig up some evidence that would explain what had happened to Frannie: something that would establish his innocence totally and indisputably.

Lost in his thoughts, his head still half swimming with fragments from the nightmarish hours up in Hillsdale, seeing the pathetic, battered, charred and maimed bodies of the three girls, the maniacal glare of Frannie, hearing again the hate-filled voice of the redneck truck-driver, Jerry didn't notice when the interconnecting door between the cars opened at the far end and slid shut again. Didn't see the attractive, jet-haired girl move down the compartment towards him. He wasn't even aware of her presence when she walked right up and stood over him, hanging onto the central pole. In fact, if she hadn't spoken, Jerry Zipkin might well have fallen into a deep, exhausted sleep, despite his desperate situation.

"Zippy," she said simply.

He looked up with a jerk. His head had been slowly nodding forward drowsily, lulled by the steady noise of the train. Slowly, he managed to focus his eyes. Alicia. She was there, smiling wistfully down at him. He returned the smile slowly, then reaching out, took her hand and pulled her down on the seat beside him. He looked deeply into her eyes, those unmatchable, warm, indigo pools of gentleness, then at the full, slightly parted, hesitant red lips below. And he leaned towards her and kissed her, passionately, his arms reaching around her, holding her to him, catching the delicate fragrance of her perfume as her lips yielded softly under his, her long lashes resting on her cheeks. It was a prolonged kiss that was more than a kiss because it said simply, silently and mutually: I love you. And I trust you. There was no need to put anything in words. She loved him and he loved her and he needed her so badly now, he needed her love and her trust and her strength and her warmth and her comfort. Caught up in the security and warmth of that moment, they embraced, their arms moving searchingly, fingers reaching, touching, caressing.

Then Jerry broke away, suddenly, a searing bolt of pain stabbing through his wounded shoulder. Alicia started, seeing the hurt in his face as his jaw clenched and his eyes squeezed tight to try to shut it off.

"What happened? she said, frowning.

Jerry reached his left hand over and gingerly touched his right shoulder with his fingertips. Then a sob escaped him and he leaned forward, covering his face with his hands.

"I was shot," he said, his voice muffled by the hands cupped over his face. He pulled a handkerchief from the pocket of his chinos and blew his nose, trying inconspicuously to wipe away the slight tears of self-pity that he had allowed himself.

Alicia saw and understood. She said nothing, simply took his hand and held it softly between her own.

A black woman, sitting opposite, glanced up over the top of the tabloid newspaper she was reading and eyed Jerry curiously for a moment. Jerry saw her and looked up and down the car suspiciously, then turned to Alicia.

"You sure you weren't followed?" He kept his voice low.

"Positive," she said. She looked briefly up and down the car. "You said the fifth car. This is the third."

Jerry shrugged, apologetically.

"Sorry," he said. "I can't think too straight, you know."

The train pulled in at a station and the doors opened. A uniformed cop stepped into their car. He stood right before Alicia and Jerry, hanging onto the central pole. He saw Alicia right away and was immediately aware of her striking beauty. She glanced up at him nervously and he smiled at her. She returned the smile weakly. Jerry looked down at his feet, trying to make sure the officer didn't get a good look at his face. The cop looked at Jerry, realized that the girl was with him, then moved on down the car. Jerry exhaled, relieved. Alicia touched his sleeve.

"Jerry," she said. "I...I told the police you would turn yourself in."

Jerry pursed his lips and shook his head decisively.

"You can tell them how it happened," Alicia said. "Shit, Zippy, they could tell you wouldn't kill anybody just by looking at you."

"But I did kill Frannie," Jerry said. "I pushed him in front of a goddamned truck, Alicia."

"You had to."

"I can't prove that," he said, looking earnestly into her face. "A lawyer can't prove it." He shook his head again. "I can't go to jail. I'll go crazy in jail. Even for one day. I'll go bananas."

The black woman glanced up again from her *National Enquirer*. She stared briefly at Jerry while she was turning over the pages, then she folded the newspaper to a fresh section and carried on reading.

"But running makes you look guilty," Alicia was saying. But Jerry was gazing vaguely over at the woman and her paper.

"This Lieutenant Jennings from upstate's come down here just looking for you," she went on. "They have you pegged as a psycho case."

Jerry extended his palm, the fingers of his hand spread wide.

"Frannie acted like a monster," he said. "He was no goddamned monster. Something made him act like that."

"What *could* make anyone act like that?" Alicia said, looking bewildered.

Jerry sighed with frustration, rubbing a hand over his jaw. He had the beginnings of a thick stubble. "I don't know," he said. "He was always getting these bad headaches. I thought he was a hypochondriac. But I guess something was really wrong."

He glanced again at the woman opposite reading the newspaper and, on the page facing him, the page she had just been reading, a few words of a headline caught his eye. He looked carefully. As far as he could tell, it was about someone going berserk and a mass killing. There was a photograph...no, two of them. One of bloodstained sheets covering four bodies. Another of a man, a man who had something vaguely familiar about him.

Jerry squinted, trying to take in more detail, but just then the woman folded her paper and got up. The train was approaching a station. Jerry got up, too, as the car slowed to a gradual stop and the doors slid open.

He turned to Alicia and said quickly:

"I'll call you. Don't try to reach me—I'll call you."

"I want to come!" she said, startled, rising from her seat. He whirled and kissed her swiftly on the lips, then turned and jumped off the train. She stepped forward to follow but the doors slid closed in her face. She kicked frustratedly at the bottom paneling as she watched Jerry's back retreating along the platform and the train pulled out.

On the station, Jerry walked over to a newsstand and bought a copy of the *National Enquirer*. Standing there on the platform as the train moved away, he feverishly turned the pages, looking for the article he wanted. He found it.

The headline, in large, black, jump-out type, said:

DETECTIVE GOES MAD, KILLS WIFE, TWO CHILDREN
AND NEIGHBOR — THEN KILLS SELF.

A smaller, second-deck heading added:

EVEN NEIGHBOR'S DOG NOT SPARED NIGHT OF TERROR.

Quickly, Jerry read the article. It had happened in a New York suburb called Valley Stream. Beside the broad block of type were the two pictures. The large one with the four bodies and the sheets over them and the obvious bloodstains. And an insert, a circular close-up of a man's face. It had been that photograph and the "GOES MAD" phrase in the headline that had attracted Jerry's attention on the train. The insert photograph was of the alleged murderer and suicide case. Not only had the man gone mad and slaughtered his own family, a neighbor and his dog. *He was completely bald and had wide, wild, staring eyes. Just like Frannie Scott.*

CHAPTER 10

IT DIDN'T TAKE LONG for Jerry to find the neatly landscaped, suburban development of Valley Stream. It was a cluster of modest detached and duplex houses built in about four or five different styles, all intermingled so that the streets did not look too stereotyped and uniform. The different colorings of the roof tiles added to the variational effect. There were deep browns, reds, pale blues and ordinary, slate greys.

Jerry steered his jeep down the winding street,

peering out at the houses with their short driveways, postage-stamp lawns and well-tended flowerbeds, although at present, the flowers were few and the soil was coated in February frost. He did not really know exactly what he was looking for in coming here, where a bald young detective had gone berserk. But there *had* to be something...some connection with the fact that Frannie Scott had been bald, went mad and killed three girls and that Detective John O'Malley had also been bald and an insane killer of four people and a dog.

He wondered if John O'Malley had complained of headaches, like Frannie. There had to be some kind of connection; the kind that the cops would hardly be in a position to link up. Why should they look for correspondences between two separate murder cases, one in a ski house up in Hillsdale, the other in a relatively built-up, quiet residential suburb?

Jerry felt certain that, whatever the connection might be, he had to find it. Oddly, intuitively, he was convinced that it was the only thing that might help him to establish his own innocence.

He chose one of the Valley Stream houses at random: a comfortable-looking, red Cape Cod-style dwelling. He pulled over to the curb, parked the jeep and got out. He walked up the short driveway, tugging up the collar of his overcoat against the biting cold wind, and rang the doorbell.

There was no answer. He rang again. The house had that empty feeling. He could hear no sounds inside and nobody came to the door. He cut across the lawn of the house next door and tried there. In a few seconds, a middle-aged woman with red hair and a timid, worried face like a squirrel, cautiously opened the door. She was wearing a knitted, zip-fronted sweater and a pair of bottle-green slacks. The sweater was chunky and served to hide her drooping, bra-less breasts. But she shouldn't have worn slacks. She was too broad in the beam and her belly sagged.

"Yes?" she said, eyeing Jerry.

"Hi," he said, smiling, hoping she wouldn't look too carefully at his forty-eight-hour stubble and the griminess of the overcoat with the small bullet holes and rust-brown stains in the right shoulder.

"Yes? she said again.

"I... uh…heard about what happened next door."

"You a reporter?" She scowled. "I've said all I plan on saying, thank you."

She went to close the door, but Jerry spoke again. quickly.

"No—I'm not a reporter," he said. "I'm not a reporter. Was it your husband who was killed?"

She opened the door again and stepped in front of it.

"I tried to ring next door," Jerry said, jerking a thumb at the house he'd come from. "But nobody answers."

"It wasn't my husband," the woman said. "It was Richard Grosso, the neighbor on the other side."

"Why would a guy go and kill all those people?" Jerry said. "Why'd he do it?"

She stared suspiciously at Jerry again, looking him right up and down.

"You a cop?" she asked, dubiously. You never knew, these days. Some of those undercover men, they dressed up like winos and hippies and everything.

Jerry shook his head.

"Did you know Johnny?" she asked.

"No," Jerry said. "It said in the paper he killed a dog, too?"

She gave him the once-over again and, for no particular reason that she could put her finger on, decided he was all right. She didn't know who he was, this somewhat scruffy individual, standing on her doorstep, and he didn't seem eager to be telling. But the way he looked at her, all open faced and innocent, asking questions like a kid. He seemed okay. Maybe he was a relative, poor guy, and too ashamed to admit it. It wasn't easy to admit that one of your family, one of your own flesh and blood, had gone haywire and turned killer. She made up her mind. She leaned forward and said, quietly:

"Richie, that's Richard Grosso, the man who was killed, he heard screaming coming from the O'Malleys'. He took his dog, Shep, one of those police dogs, and went to see what it was all about. I was the one who finally called the cops. That was after I'd heard a gun go off."

"Gun?"

"You're not a reporter?" Jerry shook his head again.

The woman looked up and down the street. It was deserted. She had a distinctive way about her; she was a classifiable type, Jerry thought. Sort of frayed middle-class. Probably with a middle-class American name. She looked like an Emily or an Agnes or even an Alice. Someone's aunt.

She leaned close again, as if she were about to disclose some earth-shattering secret—even though she had already told the cops three times and the newspapermen five times.

"When the cops arrived," she said, "they found Richard Grosso lying dead on the steps. His neck was broken. And upstairs they found all the O'Malleys lying dead in big red pools of blood. Johnny put a bullet through his own head, the others..."

She shook her head and closed her eyes, frowning distastefully, as if she couldn't bear to think about what happened to the others, let alone describe it.

"The dog?" said Jerry.

"Old Shep? His jaws were broken wide opened, bent all the way back, like this."

She made a pair of jaws with cupped hands, then opened them wide and twisted the upper hand to one side. Then she shuddered.

"Could I get in there?" Jerry asked, wondering if the woman had been neighborly enough to have been entrusted with a key.

"You an insurance adjuster?" the woman said, looking doubtfully again at Jerry's shabby appearance.

He gave her a thin smile, as if to say: Do I look like an insurance man?

"Well you won't be able to get in there. They got it locked up good. I sure wouldn't want to set foot in there."

She glanced down the street towards the O'Malley place.

"Johnny was the gentlest thing with those kids," she said. "I never thought he'd make it as a detective. I thought he'd be too soft. I guess you never know what's going on inside people's heads, do you?"

"I guess not," Jerry said. "One more thing. Could you tell me when John O'Malley lost his hair?"

"You know," the woman said, laying a hand on his arm. "That's the strangest thing. I never knew he was bald."

He thanked her and walked back to his jeep, climbed in and started the engine. She watched from her doorstep as the strange but pleasant young man drove off, seemingly out of the neighborhood, down the winding street, turning right at the T-junction. She stepped forward a few paces along her drive and glanced at the O'Malley place with its darkened, silent windows. She shuddered again, then went in and closed the door.

CHAPTER 11

Jerry did not leave the neighborhood. He turned the jeep right at the top of the street, then right again down a narrow lane that skirted a low hedgerow, backing onto the row of houses in which the O'Malley place stood. Counting the backs of the houses as he drove, looking out for the distinctive red Cape Cod, he stopped the vehicle one door up and parked it close to the hedge where it was unlikely to be seen by anyone looking out their back window. He got out, went around the back and opened the rear panel of the jeep. He took a crowbar from the tools inside, then, ducking low, he cut across the back lawn of the Grosso house until he was standing by the corner of the O'Malley place.

He found the basement window and for a few moments examined the way it was constructed, the type of frame and catch. Then he placed the tip of the crowbar in the tiny gap between the window frame and the outer-frame and tapped it gently with the heel of his hand. Gradually, the crowbar went in an inch or so until it was wedged in firmly, then he leaned on it. After a few moments, the window frame creaked, the soft metal of the latch gave and the window opened.

Jerry glanced up and down to make sure he wasn't being watched, then carefully clambered inside. The basement was cold and empty, except for a few old wooden packing cases lying in a corner and the ducts of the central heating unit bracketed to the wooden beams of the ceiling. The unit itself was set against a wall. It was silent and had obviously been turned off when the police sealed the house.

Lighting matches as he went, Jerry wandered around the basement until he found the wooden staircase leading up into the rest of the house. He cautiously ascended, testing each stair with his foot before putting his weight on it and eventually made it to the top. He opened the door into the main, ground floor and paused, listening. There was no sound in the place, so he continued on along the hall and into the living room. His breath hung in vaporous clouds on the freezing cold air.

The living room showed no signs of a struggle of any kind. The furniture was intact and all in place and the room seemed neat and tidy. On the mantel above the fireplace was a framed family photograph: the O'Malleys. A man, his wife and two young boys standing in front of them, their parents' hands on their shoulders. John O'Malley was smiling quietly into the camera and Jerry noticed that he seemed to have a normal, full head of hair. He certainly did not look like the kind of guy who'd go berserk and slaughter his own family.

He headed off towards the staircase and was about to go up when he started back, his heart thumping. There on the hallway carpet and partly on the lower two stairs, was the sprawled figure of a man.

Then, he realized. It was an outline in chalk made by Homicide detectives to mark the position of a body. Jerry took a deep breath to steady his nerves. In spite of the chilly atmosphere in the deserted house he found his forehead breaking out in perspiration and his shirt clinging uncomfortably to his body. Stepping carefully to avoid walking on the chalk marks, he went upstairs.

First, he found the children's bedroom, with a large jumble of toys strewn about the place; on the beds, on chairs, on the window-ledge, everywhere. Not the normal clutter of a kids' playroom, but a violent scattering as if someone had deliberately hurled things about, in a rage or a panic. There were boys' clothes, tattered and shredded, lying everywhere, too, as if they had been thrown. On the floor were two more chalked figures, miniatures of the one he had encountered downstairs. The outlines of the two boys, where they had fallen dead.

Jerry closed his eyes, his breath quickening. He could almost hear the agonized screams of the two boys as they were stalked about the room and attacked savagely by their demented father. Somewhere in the background, there would have been a woman, screaming hysterically, horribly. He thought of the attractive young woman in the photograph downstairs. There would have been another man's voice eventually, too, the neighbor, screaming and yelling in shock and terror, his dog barking and snarling furiously as it tried to save its master. Then, even the dog would have howled and yelped in agony as its limbs were torn by powerful hands, its jaws wrenched apart in an obscene death rictus.

Jerry moved away from the children's room and on to the master bedroom at the front of the house. In the back of his mind, he still heard that hideous cacophony of screaming—children, woman, man and dog—echoing away across the otherwise still, moonlit gardens of Valley Stream. He imagined himself face to face with John O'Malley, the madman, as he had been confronted by Frannie. The bald head and the charcoal black, lunatic staring saucer eyes, the hideous, sadistic, cracked smile of utter insanity. He saw himself grabbing hold of that grinning figure, tightly around the throat, then smashing its head mercilessly, time and time again against the hardwood floor. But that was not the way it had been. A gunshot, fired by the maniac's own hand, had cracked out sharp and sudden in the night and the dead, black eyes of John O'Malley were finally dead for real.

Jerry came out of his almost hallucinatory mental re-enactment of the sickening drama in the O'Malley house of horror, to find that he was utterly saturated in perspiration and his heart was thumping wildly. He opened his eyes and looked down to see the chalked figure on the floor of the master bedroom where John O'Malley had fallen when he finally took his own life. Why? Why did he go mad? Why did he lose his hair? What was the common factor? There had to be something.

Jerry went over to a chest of drawers and rummaged around inside. He pulled out two male wigs, full hairpieces, longish and reddish-brown in color. The reasons why no doubt, the lady next door and maybe all the neighbors for that matter, had no idea that John O'Malley, Detective Second Class, was totally bald. Jerry wondered if the cops down at O'Malley's precinct had even known that he was bald…until his death. That photograph in the *Enquirer*; it could well have been a morgue shot, one of those pictures where they do a head-and-shoulders of the corpse, right there on the slab, trying to make it look as lifelike as possible. It was a macabre but necessary method of providing a recent likeness when no others were available.

"Hey you!"

Jerry froze and his heart leapt into his mouth as the harsh, strident voice rang out suddenly. He whirled around, fully expecting to see some patrolman standing in the doorway, signifying that his little amateur detective game was over.

But there was no one there. His heart hammering against his ribcage, Jerry quickly looked around the room. There was no one. He looked at the window, thinking perhaps that it might have been open and that he might have heard a cry from the street below. But the window was closed. And anyway, the voice had seemed much closer, in the room with him.

Then he heard the scratching. It seemed to come from a closet in the corner.

God! he thought. Maybe there was someone locked in there, someone who might have hidden when O'Malley went on the rampage and had been in there ever since, terrified or unable to get out. A neighbor's kid, perhaps. Possibly someone injured.

He walked stealthily over to the closet, reached out, took the handle and slowly turned it. He eased the door open gradually. The closet was dark and hung with clothes and he could not see into its shadowy recesses. He stood there a moment, waiting to see if anyone would emerge, or whether the voice would cry out again. But there was only silence and the hammering of his heart.

Then suddenly, from the shelf above the rail of clothes there was a fearful, eerie noise, a shrill, high-pitched screech, accompanied by a terrible, dazzling flash of color. Instinctively, Jerry threw up his hands to protect himself and felt a sudden flurry and a draught on his face. For a moment he felt like he was going to faint dead away in terror.

He stumbled backward and the backs of his legs came up against the edge of the bed. Off-balance, he fell awkwardly into a sitting position on the mattress, flinging out his arms to save himself. As he did so, he looked across the room, his face still frozen with fear.

A large, blue and green macaw was perching calmly on a small desk by the bedroom window.

"Phew!"

Jerry's sigh of relief was so sudden and spontaneous, it startled even himself momentarily. He drew a hand across his forehead and it came away drenched with perspiration. The macaw began to flap its wings again and with a flurry, it launched itself from the desk to land on the side of a birdcage that was lying overturned near the desk.

"Hey you!" the macaw screeched, in its grating, near-human voice. "Hey you!"

Jerry got up and went over to the bird. He put out a hand and it clambered onto his wrist. With his other hand he picked up the cage and set it upright on the desk. Then he thrust the bird through the open door and it clambered back onto its perch, watching him with its large round eyes that were surrounded with wrinkled grey flesh.

"Hello Johnny, hello Johnny. Hey you!" it squawked loudly.

"Shhhhhhhh!" Jerry said, placing a finger to his lips, afraid that the parrot's raucous voice might attract the attention of neighbors. But the macaw did not seem to understand such gestures.

"Hey you! Hey you!" it went.

Jerry happened to glance at the desk at that moment, wondering if there was anything there that might provide a clue to the mystery of the bald-headed madman. Hanging on the wall beside the desk in a frame was a college diploma. Jerry looked closer. It said that John O'Malley had graduated from Syracuse University in 1967. And bells began to ring in Jerry's brain. Frannie Scott went to Syracuse and graduated in 1967. He went bald and went mad. So did John O'Malley.

But what was the significance of that? The macaw gave him the next clue.

In what could only be a parody of the voice of the late John O'Malley, possibly even during his final, tormented moments, before he put the gun to his temple, the macaw shrieked:

"Blue Sunshine...no more!"

"Blue Sunshine...no more?"

And left Jerry as puzzled as ever.

CHAPTER 12

JERRY FIGURED that if the whole of the New York Homicide, plus an upstate detective, were against him, looking out for him to book him for murder, turning into an amateur cracksman was pretty small apples. Which was why he had no compunction about going downtown to Frannie Scott's small, lockup photographic studio and busting in for a snoop around.

Besides, it might even save his neck, if he found some interesting evidence. As he drove the Bronco jeep all the way back downtown from the Valley Stream suburb, Jerry had been racking his brain over that phrase that the macaw had yelled. What the hell did it mean? Somehow, "Blue Sunshine" seemed vaguely, but extremely vaguely, familiar. It sounded like the title of an old 'fifties country and western number or something. Jerry just could not put his finger on where he'd heard it before. It might have been at college, but he couldn't be sure. Could it, he wondered, have been the name of some secret society that Frannie and O'Malley had belonged to? Maybe a black magic sect whose members shaved their heads. But even if that were so, how did it link in with the madness and the murders? One thing he did know: he definitely had heard the phrase before.

Blue Sunshine. It could be anything: a new washing powder, or shampoo, the title of a science fiction novel, the name of a pop group, or even a popular tag for an advanced form of ultra-violet radiation treatment in a sauna bath. But which, if any, of those would have been capable of (a) causing sudden baldness, (b) driving people mad, and (c) causing psychopathic killer tendencies?

The first thing that confronted Jerry when he had finally jimmied open the door of Frannie's studio was a giant blow-up of Frannie, pointing a determined finger at him and glowering from beneath knotted eyebrows. Frannie was dressed up, in the photograph, as Uncle Sam, with white wig, top hat, moustache and goatee in the classic Uncle-Sam-needs-you pose. Jerry closed the door quietly behind him and switched on the studio lights.

There was a whole row of photographs mounted and framed along the narrow wall. The first batch were in black and white, grainy, arty stuff of wizened old men huddled in Skid Row doorways with vacant, hollow eyes; poor black kids in the stinking summer streets, taking a showerbath under the spray from a burst fire hydrant; willowy model girls in strange, angular, unnatural poses that belonged to the days of the mini-skirt, maxi-boots, and hot pants. There were even some modelling shots of Alicia, before Jerry had known her, in various attractive poses. Next to that section was a shot of Alicia and Jerry, looking very happy, arm-in-arm, laughing in the sunshine of a park with trees and a duckpond in the background.

Then came the color shots. These must have been taken during the time when Frannie was at college, mixing with the weirdies down in the Village and experimenting with all kinds of strange lenses, filters and distorted fish-eye effects. The faces and figures of the bizarre, outrageously clad figures in these pictures were all warped with hazy filters and angle-shots that made facial features and limbs look grotesquely old fashioned, foreshortened or elongated. Jerry peered closely at the photographs as he moved along.

The young men and women were virtually indistinguishable: the girls all scrawny and flat-chested with short, short hairdos and strange designs like stars and crescents and other odd shapes painted on their faces and bodies. The sad, sick, left-over kids of the psychedelic era. The boys were all hairy and effeminate, standing in gawkish, girlish poses, mincing and winking coyly with hands on hips and eye makeup laid on heavily. It was a mini exhibition that reflected the New York version of the San Francisco flower-power period after it had wilted. The photographic techniques were superb. But the actual subject matter was often hellish and hideous, the nightmarish world of a decadent, over-fed, overpaid, bored drug generation. Jerry paused at one of the pictures and stared hard.

It showed a freaky young guy with a cluster of colorful beads around his neck. He was bare-chested with long wild hair, apparently lifted into a halo, a jagged swirl around his head, by the wind. His face was deathly pale as if he'd never seen the sun, almost like that of an albino, or a hemophiliac. His wild, tawny hair was a most unnatural silvery blue, either dyed or sprayed. His eyes were staring like a madman, his face distorted, mouth opened wide as if he were screaming in the midst of some bad acid trip, trying to scare off the demons of his own drug-induced private hell.

There was a small, printed caption at the base of the photograph. Jerry leaned closer to read it. It said:

BLUE SUNSHINE

Jerry stared intently again at the features of the young man in the picture. Stared until he was absolutely sure. The subject had changed a lot over the ten or so years since the photograph was taken. But there was no doubt about it. The young, wild, freaky acidhead in the picture was none other than Edward Flemming, congressional candidate.

CHAPTER 13

EDWARD FLEMMING'S mobile campaign headquarters was, as usual, buzzing with activity, almost like an army field HQ out on maneuvers. There were smartly turned-out girls outside, half-a-dozen or more of them, stuffing leaflets into the hands of passers-by on the parking lot of the multi-story shopping complex where the cream-colored trailer was parked. Others were adding tubular framed chairs to the ones already arranged in neat rows in front of the platform and microphone that had been assembled near the trailer. Two technicians were crawling under the platform, checking the wiring, and another, wearing headphones, was testing the sound system. Inside the trailer, which was decked out like an office, with files and folders, typewriters and in/out trays and a clutch of telephones that seemed to ring incessantly, other paid helpers were making last-minute arrangements, correcting speech typescripts, calling up future venues where the would-be Congressman was due to speak. Even Flemming himself, looking uncharacteristically flustered, was on the phone.

The only trouble was, there were only three or four people sitting out there, waiting for the great man to come out and address them.

That was why Edward Flemming was looking harassed.

That was why, right now, a few minutes before he was due to speak, he was still on the phone.

Wayne Mulligan, Flemming's campaign manager, entered the trailer. He had just been around the shopping center, checking that all the familiar, Flemming-Is-The-Future posters were prominently displayed. As he waited for Flemming to finish talking on the phone, Wayne, a tall, husky, athletic type of about twenty-seven, ducked down to look in 3 mirrors on the wall, teasing his long blond hair into place with his fingertips.

"What kind of organization do we have?" Flemming was shouting angrily into the phone. "There's about six people out there!"

Finished with his hair, Wayne caught Flemming's eye and made a circle with forefinger and thumb, signaling that he had some good news. Still glowering, Flemming spoke impatiently into the phone again.

"Wait a minute," he told the person at the other end. "Yeah, Wayne?"

"Great news," Wayne said. "We got the Shopper's World Mall for the big rally."

Flemming's expression brightened and he nodded his approval. They had been trying to get one of the prominent concessions on the main aisle at the Shopper's World center for three weeks. It was the world's largest shopping complex and Flemming was counting on speaking there, knowing that thousands of people would be attracted: the kind of people he wanted to impress; young, potential supporters who would come to the place to look at home fixtures, clothing and furniture.

"Hear that?" Flemming said into the phone. "We're okay for the Shopper's World thing. The Mall. Okay? Yeah… send as many as you can. And voting age. Got it? Right."

He hung up the receiver.

One of the women campaign workers waved a sheet of typed foolscap paper at Flemming from her desk down at one end of the trailer, trying to gain his attention. But Wayne stepped in front of her line of vision and took Flemming's arm.

"Some guy outside wants to talk to you," he said.

"What's his name?"

"Jerry Zipkin, I think."

Flemming crossed over to the window, pushed the orange curtain to one side and peered out. He saw the tall, scruffy-looking figure of Jerry standing leaning on his jeep, which was parked to the left of the fenced-off area where the chairs were set out.

"Did he say what he wanted?" Flemming said, still studying Jerry thoughtfully.

"Just to see you."

Flemming sighed. It didn't do to turn people away, whatever they wanted; especially not if they were potential voters.

"Okay," he said. "Send him over."

Wayne went to the door. The woman at the desk called out to Flemming, now that he seemed to be disengaged.

"Mr. Flemming?"

He looked at her, raising a quizzical eyebrow.

"I'm going ahead with the puppet show, now that we nailed down Shopper's World," she said.

Flemming flashed her his toothpaste-ad, showbiz smile.

"Absolutely," he said.

Wayne opened the trailer door and beckoned Jerry to come over. For the first time, he caught a glimpse of the girl that was with Flemming's visitor. Alicia stood by the jeep, watching Jerry's retreating back, then wandered off across the parking lot. From what Wayne could see of her, she looked a real honey.

He backed away from the open door as Jerry came up and poked his head inside. Jerry quickly spotted Flemming and spoke.

"Hi! I'm Jerry Zipkin. Can I talk to you for just a second?"

"Sure," Flemming said, giving Jerry a fleeting burst of his professional smile. "What is it?"

"Alone," Jerry said, looking at the other people inside the trailer.

Flemming glanced at Wayne and rolled up his eyes. What was this, another nut?

"I'm...really tied up now," Flemming said apologetically to Jerry, sweeping an arm to indicate the busy atmosphere of the trailer, taking it all in, the clattering typewriters, the buzzing telephones.

"It's important," Jerry said. "It won't take long." Flemming shrugged, shot another glance at Wayne with a wink that said: If I'm not back in five, come and rescue me.

He stepped out of the trailer and fell in step beside Jerry, walking towards the jeep.

"Did you know a guy named Francis Scott?" Jerry asked.

"Frannie? Sure. Hey, how is he?" Flemming said. "I haven't seen Frannie Scott in...wait." He looked Jerry in the eyes. "What do you mean, *did* I know?"

"Frannie's gone," Jerry said.

Flemming studied Jerry's face to see what he meant by "gone". Jerry nodded grimly. Flemming looked quite genuinely shocked.

Just then, two middle-aged men in business suits and carrying briefcases came up and barged in without even looking at Jerry. Flemming excused himself and shook their hands. Jerry lit up a cigarette and waited, impatiently, leaning on the door of his jeep.

Over by the long trailer, Alicia was on patrol, just like Jerry had asked her. She was glancing around casually as she strolled along, keeping an eye out in case the law showed up. Wayne Mulligan was looking out of the window of the trailer at her. He'd been right, he was telling himself, the girl was a looker all right. He went back to the mirror on the wall and gently ran a comb through his hair. Then he tugged down the hem of his sports jacket, straightening it, brushed at his grey slacks with his hand and stepped outside.

"Hi!" Wayne showed her his big, friendly, ex-college boy's clean-cut grin.

"Hi," Alicia said, distractedly.

"Voting for Ed Flemming?" he asked, his hands in his pockets, falling into step with her. Alicia shrugged and made a slight face.

"Sure," she said unconvincingly. "Why not?"

"That's not a very healthy voter attitude," Wayne said.

"I really don't know much about him. Do you?"

"Over ten years," Wayne said proudly, as if he were telling her he'd known somebody real big for ten years, like Bing Crosby or the President.

"We went to Syracuse together," he added, watching to see if she was impressed. "I...uh, played a little football there. Ever hear of big number thirty-two, Wayne Mulligan?"

Alicia shook her head.

"Sorry," she said.

"Well, that's me," Wayne said, unabashed, prodding his thumb in his chest. If this chick hadn't heard of him before, he was going to do his best to make sure she'd hear of him in the future. He couldn't take his eyes off her.

"Oh," Alicia said, vaguely, still looking warily around for signs of the police. And she was thinking: What a creep. Why doesn't he get lost?

"And you're ..."

"Alicia Sweeny," she said, then added, pointedly, "I'm waiting for Jerry."

She looked over to where Jerry was standing beside the jeep while the two men were talking to Edward Flemming. Wayne followed her gaze, sizing up Jerry briefly, then taking the opportunity to have a good look at Alicia's figure while she wasn't looking. His eyes travelled down from the soft, white lines of her neck to her blouse, where the full, firm breasts thrusted against the material. She was not wearing a bra and her nipples showed quite clearly. Her denim flares were tight-fitting around her hips and thighs and he tried to imagine the soft warmth between them, where her body curved inwards and under.

Had she been paying attention, Alicia would probably have felt Wayne's eyes intimately roaming over her body. But she was still staring at Jerry. Flemming seemed to have finished talking to the two men, he was shaking hands and taking his leave of them.

"Sorry," Flemming said, turning back to Jerry. "What was it? Accident?"

Jerry shook his head.

"What happened?"

"I'm not sure," Jerry said. "Something kind of came over him. Some kind of disease."

He studied Flemming's features, trying to detect any flicker of reaction. But he was distracted by the sight of a man in the distance, on the other side of the parking lot. The stranger was leaning against the side of a blue Chevrolet Monte Carlo, looking around carefully. He seemed to be searching for someone among the shoppers moving to and fro over the large parking lot.

Jerry had never seen Lieutenant Jennings before in his life, but he could tell the man was a cop, just by the way he was standing there, watching.

Flemming noticed Jerry's sudden nervousness, the furtive darting eyes, the way he was clasping and unclasping his hands.

"Gee… Frannie Scott," Flemming said. "That's a shame."

A woman called out from the direction of the trailer.

"Mr. Flemming! I have the puppet people on the phone. They want to talk to you."

"In a minute" Flemming called. He turned to Jerry.

"Well, I guess that's it, then."

"There's more," Jerry said earnestly, his eyes boring into the politician's face. "Frannie had a picture of you in his studio."

Flemming smiled, raising an eyebrow as if to say: So what?

"That's not surprising," he said. "He used to snap away at anything. He was damned good at it, too."

"But this was different," Jerry said. "It was all distorted, like the vision of a madman."

Flemming shrugged his shoulders, not quite understanding what Jerry was getting at. Jerry flashed another glance at the man by the parked Monte Carlo. He was lighting a cigarette. Jerry quickly turned his face away in case the man saw him.

"Ed," Jerry said. "Did you ever hear of Blue Sunshine?"

Flemming tensed and glanced around nervously.

Jerry noticed his reaction.

"It was the caption under this picture of you," Jerry said. "I thought you might know what it meant."

"Never heard of it," Flemming said, too quickly.

"Mr. Flemming!" The woman was calling from the trailer again. "Do you want political caricatures or show-business personality-type puppets?"

"Nothing political," Flemming called. Then he saw his opportunity. "I really have to go now," he said, turning to Jerry.

He started to move away, but Jerry grabbed his arm.

"Wait," he said. "You see, this disease that Frannie had.... I don't know, it was just a hunch...but I thought Blue Sunshine might have something to do with it."

Flemming wheeled on him. He was losing his patience.

"Well I don't know what you're talking about," he said. "I'm sorry to hear about your friend. Now if you'll kindly let go of my arm."

"Any problem here, Ed?"

Jerry turned his head to see the burly figure of Wayne Mulligan towering over him. Jerry let go of Flemming's arm. He glanced across the parking Jot and saw Alicia talking to the man he'd seen leaning against the Monte Carlo. The man was looking around rapidly, as if searching for someone.

"Please," Jerry said to Flemming, "anything you can tell me..."

"There's nothing to tell you," Flemming said coldly.

Jerry took his arm again. Wayne reached out and, with the slightest effort, removed Jerry's fingers from the politician's forearm. Then he placed a hand on Jerry's chest and shoved, sending him staggering backwards a few paces.

The slight altercation was not lost on Lieutenant Jennings. He guessed from Alicia's look of concern that the man being pushed aside by one of Flemming's henchmen must be the man he was looking for. He started to move off, but Alicia took hold of his arm.

"Lieutenant, listen," she said.

When Jennings turned to her, Alicia saw Jerry dart away from Mulligan and Flemming, sprinting across the pavement to his jeep. Jennings looked around, saw what was happening and broke away from Alicia, heading for his own car.

With a screech of tires, Jerry peeled out of the parking lot, as Jennings was putting his keys in the ignition of the Monte Carlo.

Wayne and Flemming stood looking on. "What was all that about?" Wayne said.

"I'm not sure," Flemming said, putting a hand on Wayne's shoulder and steering him back towards the trailer. "But we'd better keep a close eye on Mr. Zipkin. He could be a trouble-maker." As they neared the rows of seats in front of the plat-form, there were still only half-a-dozen or so shoppers there, waiting for Flemming to deliver his speech. Wayne paused to watch the blue Monte Carlo speeding out of the parking lot.

The Chevrolet was faster, much faster than the Bronco jeep and Jerry knew it. But he had the slight advantage of a four-wheel drive. He cut back around the periphery of the shopping plaza, then wheeled into the parking lot again. He could hear the screeching tires of the Monte Carlo as it cornered, hard in pursuit.

At that moment, Wayne had mounted the small platform in front of the campaign trailer and was introducing Edward Flemming to the almost negligible audience out front.

"Ladies and Gentlemen," he said. "Our next Congressman—Edward Flemming."

Flemming stepped up to the microphone to the weakest ripple of applause of his whole political career. Beaming broadly, as if there were ten thousand people out there, he raised his arms, as if to stem a deafening tide of welcoming cheers and applause.

He opened his mouth to speak, but no words came out as the screech of tires shrieked out over the parking lot. Flemming coughed nervously, then began.

"We have a responsibility," he said, falteringly, "a responsibility..."

He paused as he saw the jeep double back on its tracks, weaving dangerously between shoppers who were moving slowly across the parking lot, pushing carloads of groceries. Others were backing their cars in and out of the spaces on the lot. The little jeep wove its way in and out of them deftly, the blue Monte Carlo swayed on its suspension as it tried to follow.

"...a responsibility to our, uh, elderly," Flemming went on, unable to take his eyes off the car chase. "A responsibility which, I'm sad to say, we're not living up to..."

He saw the jeep cut down the ramp out of the lot and into the stream of traffic on the highway that sliced past the shopping center. The Monte Carlo followed. Trying at the same time to concentrate on his speech, Flemming wondered what the hell was going on.

Alicia was standing at the rear of the fenced-off seating area, chewing nervously on a finger and wondering whether Jennings would catch up with Jerry. And if he did, would Jerry think that she had deliberately led him into a trap?

The road beyond the shopping center was a dual highway, divided by a steep, grassy embankment. Jerry pressed his foot to the floorboards, but the Monte Carlo was gaining on him. Within seconds, the detective's car was alongside. Jennings rolled down his window.

"Pull over!" he yelled.

Jerry ignored him, looking straight ahead, his pedal to the floor.

Jennings swung his wheel to the left, sideswiping the jeep, trying to nudge it off the road. For a moment, Jerry wrestled with his steering wheel, trying to keep his vehicle on a straight course. The Monte Carlo fell back.

Jennings reached into his shoulder holster for his .38 revolver. He accelerated to get within close range, but just then Jerry slammed the four-wheel drive into low gear and yanked the wheel to the left, turning the jeep sharply off the road, bouncing up the steep dividing meridian.

Like an insect, the jeep, its engine roaring, gripped the steep grassy bank, reaching the top within seconds. Jennings' car had overshot the place by the time Jerry reached the top, swung on the wheel and filtered neatly into the traffic travelling in the opposite direction.

For the second time in forty-eight hours, Lieutenant Jennings cursed television for all the smart-assed tricks it was teaching people, especially kids like Jerry Zipkin.

CHAPTER 14

THEY MET on the subway again, but in Manhattan. It seemed the safest place. Surrounded by commuters, Jerry and Alicia huddled together, hanging on to the central pole of the car. Behind Alicia, a passenger stubbornly tried to read his newspaper, despite the fact that he had difficulty in the confined space in turning over the pages.

"What did Flemming say?" Alicia asked.

"He knew Frannie all right," Jerry said.

"And Blue Sunshine?"

Jerry smiled grimly.

"He was a real sweety until I brought that up. Then he acted like I was a known swine flu carrier. I can't figure out why."

Alicia looked puzzled for a moment as she tried to order her thoughts.

"Okay," she said. "Frannie, O'Malley and now Flemming all went to Syracuse ten years ago..."

"What?" Jerry said, surprised. "Flemming went to Syracuse? How do you know?"

"Some big guy that works for him told me," Alicia said. "They both graduated ten years ago."

Jerry shut his eyes momentarily. As the subway train rattled and roared on beneath the city streets, he re-lived for a fleeting instant, a moment from his last visit to Dr. Blume's office. He remembered Blume's graduation diploma on the wall...and the strand of hair that he had picked up from the doctor's desk. And Blume's obvious embarrassment.

Jerry opened his eyes and found himself looking straight in the face of the bald-headed man, the stubborn commuter with the newspaper. Alicia turned to see what Jerry was staring at and the bald man self-consciously buried his face in his paper.

"Davie..." Jerry said, almost to himself.

"What?" Alicia looked at him, uncomprehendingly. "Zippy. Davie who?"

Jerry thought for a moment, then came to a decision.

"I better not tell you," he said. "You're in enough trouble already."

"I don't care," Alicia said. She wanted him to trust her. In everything to do with this weird and perplexing affair.

But Jerry moved off towards the door, shouldering his way through the other passengers. He stood facing the door, drumming impatiently on the window pane with his fist.

Alicia quickly followed and joined him. She touched his elbow.

"But where are you going?" she said.

Jerry turned and placed his hands on her shoulders reassuringly.

"Believe me," he said, looking directly into her eyes. "Trust me. It's really better this way."

"That's not fair, Zippy," she said. "I want to help you." She sniffed girlishly and looked down at her hands. Jerry raised her chin and looked into her face again. Her eyes were beginning to brim with tears.

"You're right," he said. "You're right. Okay...listen. Eddie Flemming is hiding something about Blue Sunshine. So try to find someone else, a close friend, a girl friend, anybody who knew him in school...anything."

The rumble of the train grew louder as it slowed and drew into a station.

"I'll get in touch with you," Jerry said.

Alicia smiled. Jerry got off the train and turned to wave briefly. Then the doors closed again and the train moved off.

The fifth-floor receptionist at the hospital was pretending to read *Playgirl* magazine when Jerry walked in from the elevator. She looked up and recognized him immediately.

"Dr. Blume, please," he said.

"Zipkin?"

He returned her smile and nodded.

She dialed a number and spoke briefly into the telephone. Then she looked up. Jerry was tapping his fingers anxiously on the desk top.

"I'm sorry," she said. "Dr. Blume is in O.R."

"Operating?"

"I should think so."

"Which operating room?"

"You're not thinking of going in there?" the girl said, cautiously.

"No, no, of course not," Jerry said.

Before she could speak again, he turned and walked off towards the elevator. She watched him warily, not quite sure what he was up to.

While Jerry was at reception, Mrs. Marie Rosella was being wheeled into the operating theater. Beneath the bright fluorescent lights, supplemented by several bell-shaded stainless-steel lamps on articulated, movable frames, Dr. Blume was pulling rubber gloves onto his antiseptic-powdered hands. Mrs. Rosella looked up at him in his green surgeon's cap and matching robe as the anesthetist slipped the rubber inhalator mask over her face. Dr. Blume reached up and pulled his facemask into place and a nurse stepped up behind him, to secure the tie-strings around the back of his head.

Then he turned and looked down at the trolley beside the operating table, making sure that all the surgical implements—razor-sharp scalpels, clamps, suture threads, forceps and swabs—were in place on the gleaming white cloth. By the time that Jerry Zipkin located the Op. Room, Mrs. Rosella had already lapsed into unconsciousness and Dr. Blume was at work. Even with the green mask covering the lower part of his face, Jerry recognized the slim figure of the surgeon as he stared through the glass observation panel in the wall of the theatre.

Dr. Blume was hunched over the prostrate figure on the operating table, his hands working swiftly away while, from time to time, a nurse dabbed at his forehead with a dampened cloth.

Above the theater, on the opposite side to the glass panel, Jerry spotted a students' observation gallery. He could see that it was entered by a door at the rear. He moved off down the corridor and turned left, hoping to make his way around to the door.

After a few moments he found it, entered the balcony and sat down beside two girl students. He looked down on the tops of the surgeons' and nurses' caps, the bell-shaped lamps and the respirator and oscilloscope equipment clustered around the operating table.

From time to time as Dr. Blume shifted his position slightly, still bending over the patient, Jerry caught a glimpse of red where the woman's abdomen had been opened and the flesh was held back by clamps. The two girls sitting next to him began to talk about the operation. They spoke quietly, but Jerry could not help overhearing.

After about fifteen minutes or so, it was more than he could take. The medical jargon of the girls, the silently intent figures bending, moving to and fro below, the hot, uncomfortable atmosphere of the place, the antiseptic odor and the nauseating sound of the equipment that automatically sucked away the excess blood, and the open torso of the white-gowned figure lying still on the table. He stood up and quietly made his way out of the gallery, heading for the elevator.

He had to find out for himself about Dr. David Blume. He had to see if his, suspicions about his old friend had any foundation. Could he, Jerry wondered, possibly be suffering from the same, strange aberrations that had turned two men mad and transformed them into deranged killers?

He made his way to Blume's office and, after letting himself in and looking around briefly, decided to hide himself in the closet. He stood there in the cool darkness of the small cubicle, a welcome contrast from the hot, antiseptic atmosphere of the operating room. He left the door slightly ajar so that he could peer out into the office. After what seemed like hours, the office door opened and Blume came in, still dressed in his surgeon's cap and gown and with the mask hanging loosely at his throat.

Blume went over to his desk, loosening the tie strings of his robe, then slipped out of it and draped it across the back of a chair. From his desk he picked up a number of X-ray plates and began holding them up to the light, one by one, examining them carefully. Next, he placed them in a large brown envelope and slid them back into a wire tray on his desk.

It was then that Blume reached up and began to remove the green surgeon's skull-cap. And Jerry held his breath. When the cap came off, revealing a fairly full head of natural black hair, except for the receding hairline, Jerry could not help heaving a quite audible sight of relief. Blume heard it and looked up, startled, towards the closet.

"What the hell?" he said, as Jerry unexpectedly stepped out.

"Hi, Davie," Jerry smiled. Casually, he wandered over and closed the open door of Blume's office.

Blume scowled at him, annoyed at the intrusion.

"What the hell are you doing, Zipkin?" he demanded.

"Davie, listen," Jerry said earnestly. "I lied to you about the bullet wound."

Blume sighed wearily.

"I figured you did," he said. "But why did you come back?"

"I had to," Jerry said. "I figured you had the disease."

Blume raised his eyebrows, not understanding. "Disease? What disease?"

"Two people lost all their hair," Jerry said, "then completely flipped out and became murderers."

"Why me?"

"They both went to Syracuse the same time you did and you're losing your hair," Jerry said.

Blume noted the seriousness in his voice and frowned.

"Who are they?"

"Frannie Scott and John O'Malley."

"Frannie Scott? He's your friend, isn't he? And John O'Malley... I think I've heard of him but I've never met him."

"How about Ed Flemming?"

"Sure," Blume said. "Eddie hit me up for some money for his campaign. I owed him a lot of favors."

"What do you mean?"

"Favors," Blume said, giving Jerry a knowing look. "You know how it was back then; Everybody had to know somebody in order to score. I knew Eddie."

Realization dawned on Jerry like a sledgehammer blow. He whistled softly under his breath, then grabbed Blume by the shoulders.

"Flemming was a dealer'" he said, surprised at the loudness of his own voice. He glanced around nervously. The door was still closed and there were only the two of them in the office.

"Hey now," Blume said, shaking his head, on the defensive. "This is just between us. Something like that would kill his chances."

Jerry nodded thoughtfully and murmured, almost to himself:

"Mmmm…that would explain his clamming up."

He took a few paces around the room, rubbing his chin, deep in thought. Then he turned, looked squarely at Blume and asked the key question.

"Davie. Did you ever hear the words Blue Sunshine back in school?"

Dr. Blume shrugged, non-committally. "Could it be a drug?" Jerry asked.

"Could be," Blume said. "There were so many names back then for different types of LSD. Owsley Purple, Blue Cheer, Orange Sunshine…"

He closed his eyes as if searching his memory for half-forgotten incidents, names and faces during his reckless, irresponsible college days, when drug-taking was the fashionable in thing among most students. Practically everybody experimented with hallucinogens of all kinds during that hazy, sun-drenched season of flower-power and psychedelia, acid-rock bands, wild colorful clothes, beads and bells and free, open-air festivals.

"Yeah," he said thoughtfully, "now that you mention it, I do vaguely remember scoring something called Blue Sunshine."

"From Flemming?" Jerry asked.

"Most likely. He was my only source."

Jerry brought his fist down on Blume's desktop frustratedly.

"Then it couldn't have been Blue Sunshine because it had no effect on you," he said.

"But I didn't *take* it," Blume said, spreading his hands.

"Huh?"

Blume shook his head and walked over to the wall where his diplomas hung in their neat frames. He looked at his Syracuse graduation diploma, then turned back to Jerry.

"I never fooled around with acid," he said. "You never knew what you were getting. I just bought it and sold it. At a profit, of course…. Helped pay my tuition."

"Who'd you sell it to?" Jerry asked. Blume looked at him

and saw that an answer of some kind was important. He sighed and shrugged his shoulders.

"Anybody I didn't know," he said. "I never wanted to take chances on selling bad acid to a friend. Now let me get this straight. You think that people who took Blue Sunshine are suffering from alopecia totalis, followed by insanity?"

"Ala-what?" Jerry said.

"Complete loss of body hair."

"Could that be?" Jerry said, puzzled. "Could it have a delayed effect? Like a timebomb in the... uh, what d'you call it?"

"Chromosomes," Blume said thoughtfully.

"Yeah."

"It's highly improbable," the surgeon said.

"How could I prove it?" Jerry said.

"You'd have to take a blood test for genetic damage."

Jerry gritted his teeth, looking impatient and frustrated.

"*If* I could get one to cooperate," he said dubiously.

"Jerry," Blume said, taking his arm. "What does all this have to do with you?"

"Plenty, Davie," Jerry said. "Plenty."

He began to head for the door. Blume followed and caught up with him, confronting him. He still did not understand what it was all about, why Jerry should be involved. Jerry looked at him, frowning, then snapped his fingers.

"How do you stop a madman without killing him?" Jerry asked.

"I give up," Blume said, still not fully following Jerry's train of thought.

"No, really," Jerry said. He prodded a finger at Blume's chest. "If someone is totally berserk with the strength of a drowning man fighting for his life, how do you stop him?"

Blume shrugged.

"With drugs," he said.

"Drugs?"

"An injection of barbiturates—tranquilizers."

"But how do you get close enough to inject it?"

They went out and walked down the corridor, past the attractive receptionist. Jerry nodded briefly at her, then looked at Blume as the doctor explained how animals were often subdued by firing drugged pellets at them.

"Can you get me some?" Jerry asked, as the surgeon pressed the elevator button.

"What?"

"Tranquilizers," Jerry said.

"Jerry, this isn't Syracuse," Blume protested. "I can't just write prescriptions like I'm scoring drugs."

The elevator arrived and the metal doors slid quietly open.

"Yeah ..." Jerry said defeatedly. He stepped inside. Just as the doors were closing, Blume put out his leg and covered the automatic, electronic eye safety device, making the doors slide open again.

"What about Frannie?" Blume asked.

"He's dead," Jerry said.

Blume looked staggered by the news. He leaned into the elevator and whispered in Jerry's ear.

"I'll see what I can do," he said. "I can't promise anything. Okay?"

Jerry smiled thankfully.

"Okay," he said. "Thanks, Davie."

CHAPTER 15

Out in the Manhattan garment district, Edward Flemming's political campaign was proceeding fairly smoothly. While his workers moved busily among the crowds of stragglers and passers-by, handing out leaflets and lapel buttons, Flemming stood on the mobile podium, making a speech. Beside him, just to the rear Wayne Mulligan sat on a folding chair. But he was barely listening.

He was too busy studying the shapely contours of the girl campaign worker beside him on the platform. She was bending down, leaning into a large cardboard carton, picking out a fresh batch of leaflets and Vote-For-Flemming buttons. As she leaned further into the carton, her short skirt rode up the backs of her legs, revealing her panty hose.

Almost as if he didn't realize where he was, Mulligan leaned forward in his seat and, reaching out a huge hand, suddenly grasped the girl's left thigh, his fingers closing on the soft, warm flesh between her legs. The girl gasped and straightened up quickly, dropping all the leaflets and lapel buttons back into the carton.

As she turned, Mulligan's face was twisted into a disconcerting, lascivious leer that was positively evil and revolting. She tried to pull away, but he clamped his fingers more tightly around her thigh. She could feel the nylon of her panty hose beginning to give in his grasp.

Frightened by the silent, grinning tenacity of the man, the girl slapped his hand and he quickly snatched it away, tearing a portion of the nylon as he did so. Blushing to the roots of her blonde hair, the girl glanced quickly around the front of the podium. She was relieved to see that the audience had not noticed the brief, embarrassing incident.

They all appeared to be listening intently to Edward Flemming's speech.

Her eyes filling up with tears, the girl quickly darted away and ran down the steps at the rear of the platform and off towards Flemming's nearby campaign trailer. Up on the podium, Mulligan was leaning forward, his head in his hands, like a man suddenly beset with a stabbing, violent, agonizing headache.

Then, as he slowly raised his head, his eyes took on a faraway, glassy stare, gazing blankly at the fragment of nylon in his hand.

After a moment, he sat up straight and leaned back in his chair, almost as if nothing had happened. His eyes roved slowly over the audience standing out front. At the rear of the crowd he saw the movement of someone passing by. The girl, as she wove in and out of the people gathered on the edge of the sidewalk, looked familiar.

Alicia Sweeney hurried on, barely paying any attention to the street rally. She walked quickly over to the subway entrance and went down the steps.

She bought a token at the turnstile and moved off to the downtown platform, looking along the dark tunnel in the direction that the train would come. Two points of light in the distance and a low rumbling told her that it was on its way.

Alicia did not notice that she had been followed. As the train rumbled noisily into the station, the tall, husky figure of Wayne Mulligan shoved its way through the crowds toward her.

He watched her enter the subway car then climbed aboard in the next car. Then he moved down the passageway until he could see through the window of the inter-connecting door between the two cars. Alicia was standing in the center of the aisle, talking agitatedly to a young, dark-haired man. Mulligan recognized him as the guy who had called on Edward Flemming out on the shopping center parking lot. He saw Alicia hand Jerry a small piece of paper. Jerry stuffed it into his trouser pocket. At the next station, the young man alighted from the train in an obvious hurry and Alicia stood watching his retreating figure as the train pulled away.

Mulligan opened the inter-connecting door and moved down the car towards Alicia. She did not see him approach and he stood a few feet away in a clutch of other passengers, holding onto the center pole. He was perspiring heavily and darting nervous glances up and down the train. He put up a hand to wipe the film of sweat from his forehead and, as he did so, a large clump of matted hair on his brow was briefly swept to one side, revealing momentarily, his baldness beneath.

At the next station, Alicia got off the train and headed for the exit. Occasionally she glanced furtively around, as if she were checking to see if anyone was following her, but she still did not notice the tall figure doggedly plodding along behind her.

Suddenly, a large hand took hold of her arm and she wheeled, startled, looking breathless, half expecting to see Lieutenant Jennings or one of his men. Then she saw and recognized Wayne's face and heaved an obvious sigh of relief.

"Hi," he said.

"Hi," Alicia said nervously, trying to force a smile.

"On your way to work?"

"No...no, just doing some shopping," Alicia said, still trying to remember where she'd seen the man before.

He looked at her and she saw that he noticed she was not carrying any parcels.

"Uh...window shopping," she said somewhat weakly. "My taste is too expensive for my pocketbook."

"See anything you like?" Wayne said, falling into step beside her.

"Plenty," Alicia smiled.

"Good. Let's go," he said, taking her arm again and steering her towards the exit.

"Where?"

"Shopping," Wayne said. "I have a good expense account. One of the advantages when you're not getting paid."

Alicia stopped in her tracks.

"That's very thoughtful," she said. "But I really couldn't. I—"

"How's that guy?" She noticed his strange eyes boring into her.

"Which guy?"

"The guy you were with at the rally."

"Oh...I, uh, haven't seen him," she lied. "We're just good friends."

Mulligan smiled inwardly. Why was she lying?

Could it be that she liked him, maybe? He was about to speak when the draught from an express train that roared through the station sent powerful blasts of air up the exit tunnel. It whipped up the front of his hair, and, fortunately, the fixative on his scalp prevented the gust from tearing off his hairpiece. Frantically, he grabbed at it, plastering it back down with his hand, but not before Alicia had momentarily glimpsed the expanse of bald skin beneath.

Mulligan's face knotted into a grimace as the roar of the train filled his ears. He put both hands up to his face, as if he were in severe pain. Then it passed as suddenly as it had come and he straightened up, clearly embarrassed. Alicia looked away, pretending that she hadn't noticed a thing.

"Well," she said. "I really have to be going. Uh...maybe some other time, then?"

"Say, if you like window shopping," Wayne said, "we're having a big rally at Shoppers World, the world's biggest indoor shopping center."

Alicia remembered what Jerry had asked her to do; get close to someone who had known Flemming at Syracuse. Try to find out whatever she could.

"Yeah," she said. "That'd be great. When is it?"

"Monday night."

"How about if I meet you there?"

"Fine with me," Wayne said, grinning. "There's a discotheque called Peachtrees right in the Mall. I'll meet you at the bar."

Alicia felt an uneasy loathing for this big, powerful man; there was something obscenely animal about him. But she managed to force a smile.

"Monday night, then," she said.

She walked away up the subway exit steps and could almost feel the peculiar, cold, snakelike eyes of Wayne Mulligan boring unblinkingly into her back as she went.

CHAPTER 16

WENDY FLEMMING FELT EXACTLY like she looked—a wreck. She was taking the dishes out of the dishwasher. Her hair was long, a subtly different color, and her thin eyebrows had been crudely emphasized with dark eyebrow pencil. Inevitably, the television hummed and blared from the lounge, where the two Andretti kids were watching a children's show with hoots of laughter.

Wendy brushed a lock of hair from her eyes and went over to a kitchen cupboard. She was about to take out a bottle of tranquilizers when she heard Stephanie's voice from the hallway.

"You sure it's okay, honey?" Stephanie said, entering the kitchen. "It'll be a great help. I really can't clean the apartment with them underfoot."

"Don't be silly, go ahead," Wendy said, hurriedly replacing the bottle of drugs.

Just then the doorbell rang. Wendy went through to the living room where Jason and Samantha were sprawled on the floor and on out to the small entrance hall. She put her eye up to the spy-lens set in the front door. A lean, wiry, dark-haired young man was standing outside.

"Who's there?" Wendy called. Stephanie came up behind her and stood at her elbow.

"Jerry Zipkin," a voice said quietly. Jerry folded the scrap of paper that Alicia had given him, bearing Wendy Flemming's address, and replaced it in his pocket.

"Who?" Wendy called.

"Jerry Zipkin—a friend of Eddie's."

Wendy looked questioningly at Stephanie. She didn't recall the name. Stephanie peered briefly through the peephole in the door.

"Not too bad," she said quietly. "Open it."

Wendy did so and, for a moment, the two women eyed the stranger up and down.

"Hi, I'm Stephanie," said Wendy's neighbor. "I'm just on my way back to my apartment." She turned to Wendy. "You sure about the kids?"

"I'm sure."

"Well, nice meeting you," Stephanie said, nodding at Jerry, then sidled past him and across the corridor toward her own apartment. Wendy signaled Jerry to enter and they went into the living room.

"Eddie and I are divorced," she said.

"I know, I know," said Jerry.

"Samantha and Jason," she said, indicating her visitor. "This is Jerry." She turned to him. "They're Stephanie's," she explained. "This is like their second home."

Hands in his pockets, still not quite sure what to say, Jerry nervously shifted his weight from one foot to the other.

"Have some coffee? Wendy asked.

"No thanks."

She indicated the sofa and as they sat down Wendy reached for a cigarette. While she was lighting it, Jerry stared at the television program, *Sesame Street*. Wendy blew out a cloud of smoke.

"So," she said, "how's Eddie?"

Jerry turned to her.

"Not bad," he said, "not bad. I just saw him last week. I'll bet he wins it. He's a damn good salesman."

"I know," Wendy said. She stubbed out her cigarette after having taken only a few shallow drags. She was as ill-at-ease as her visitor.

"You caught me in the middle of putting away the dishes," she said, apologetically waving towards the kitchen.

"Sure, sure," Jerry said. "Go ahead."

She got up and he followed her into the kitchen. Wendy busied herself, stacking the dry dishes and placing them in the cupboard.

"Did you ever hear of some acid called Blue Sunshine?" Jerry said abruptly.

Wendy froze, stopped what she was doing, but she did not turn to face him.

"Acid," she said, rather too casually. "You mean LSD acid?"

"Yeah."

"Blue Sunshine? Never heard of it."

Again, it was too glib, too pat.

"There were so many crazy names," she said, with a nervous laugh. Then suddenly, something seemed to occur to her and she whirled on him. "Don't tell me you were trying to score from Eddie..." she began. Then she thought better of continuing and turned back to her work, wishing she hadn't said so much.

"No, no," Jerry said, trying to sound reassuring. "Nothing like that. Eddie had some acid about ten years ago, back in Syracuse. You went to Syracuse, right?"

"Just for two years," she said.

"The acid—it was called Blue Sunshine. It turned out to be really weird, I think it's making people go insane. I'm trying to find out who he sold it to."

She wheeled on him again, angrily, As she did so, several strands of her hair swung back and hooked over her ear. From where Jerry stood he could see quite clearly that the hair receded far back from the side of her face, too much for a natural hairline. She became flustered as he stared at her disbelievingly and stabbed at her hair with a trembling hand, quickly coaxing it back into place. She reached for another cigarette and, as she lit it, he noticed how her hands were trembling even more.

"Are you sure you're a *friend* of Eddie's?" she said at last, eyeing him warily.

"Well... not really a friend," Jerry began.

"Why do you want to implicate him in dealing with acid?" she said. She was looking quite annoyed. "Why bring this up now? That was ten years ago!"

"I told you," Jerry said quietly, trying to reason with her. "I just want to know who took it. I'm not trying to get him into trouble."

"I don't believe you," she said firmly and folded her arms. He made no reply, his eyes still staring at her hair.

"Didn't your mother tell you it's not polite to stare?" she snapped. Jerry looked down at the floor. Wendy took his arm and began ushering him towards the door. As she reached forward to open it, Jerry sneaked another long, hard look at her hair. Wendy spotted him doing it.

"Mr. Zipkin," she said, "Did anybody ever tell you that you make people feel very uncomfortable?"

"I'm sorry if I make you feel uncomfortable," Jerry said. "But if there's anything you could tell me, anything that would help locate—"

"I never heard of this drug you're talking about and Eddie never had anything to do with selling drugs," she cut in.

"But you said before—"

"What? I asked you if you were looking to buy drugs," she interrupted again. "Now I realize that you just want to get Eddie in trouble, to spoil his chances. I thought that crap stopped with Watergate."

She held the door open for him. "Please leave," she said.

He looked her in the face for a moment, pleadingly, hoping

that she might change her mind and be reasonable. But her expression was set and he saw that she was not going to cooperate in any way. He turned and left and Wendy slammed the door hard behind him.

She went back into the kitchen, looking tired and haggard.

"Wendy!" Jason bawled out from the living room. "Can we have hot dogs?

The strident sound of the child's voice seemed to Wendy ten times louder than it really was. She placed her hands over her ears and her face creased in pain, her body trembling. She staggered over to the cupboard, hands shaking as she reached out for the bottle of tranquilizers. But as she tried to get the top off, she fumbled and the small white pills scattered all over the floor, rolling away across the linoleum, under the 'fridge and stove. She did not notice in her rage and discomfort that one of the capsules rolled into the living room and came to rest beside Jason. He reached out, picked it up with a babyish grin and popped it into his mouth as if it were candy.

In the kitchen, her temples drumming painfully, Wendy scrabbled on her hands and knees on the floor, trying to retrieve the scattered pills and place them back in the bottle. She made hard work of the task, her hands still trembling uncontrollably.

"Beans!" Samantha shrieked from the other room. "An' beans with the hot dogs!"

"Soda! Soda!" bellowed Jason.

Their voices were amplified unnaturally and unbearably in Wendy's tortured brain. With an angry snort she reached up and tugged at her hair. The wig came off easily, revealing her completely bald head and she flung the mass of hair into the corner. Then her eyes, the pupils dilating strangely until the whole of the irises were blacked out, stared across the kitchen and alighted on a row of long, shiny carving knives, hanging gleaming from a magnetized wall-holder.

The kids were still yelling and bellowing from the living room, but their voices seemed almost remote now, as if they were echoing down a long, dark tunnel from some infernal, nether region, mockingly.

"Dr. Pepper!" Samantha cried, excitedly, watching the television again.

"Dr. Pepper!" Jason yelled, aping her.

Wendy looked down at the large, razor-sharp carving knife that she had taken from the wall. Her strange, staring, demented face was reflected back at her from the polished steel blade. But her unblinking, fathomless eyes did not recognize the image of what she had become. Her mind was in utter confusion. The drug that she had taken, ten years ago at Syracuse University, had slowly done its corrosive damage. She had gone stark raving mad.

CHAPTER 17

Jerry did not know quite what it was, but something made him change his mind as he rode down in the elevator from Wendy's twentieth-story apartment. At the ground floor he had been about to step out into the apartment block reception hall and off into the street. But he paused, staring at the row of buttons on the elevator panel before him.

Then, impulsively, he pressed the one marked 20 that would take him back up again. At first, the mechanism did not respond and Jerry began pounding on the button frantically.

A man and a woman, accompanied by a large St. Bernard dog, entered the elevator and, finally, the doors slid closed.

At that moment, the hideous, blank-eyed, deranged creature that Wendy Flemming had become was entering the living room, clutching the meat carver like a dagger. The two children were too lost in their television program to notice as she crept into the room behind them. Then, Jason looked up and saw the weird, death-white, hairless apparition standing over him. He stared for a moment, his eyes wide and innocent. Then he began to laugh, pointing at her, as if she were made up like a circus clown. Samantha glanced up and also began to laugh. The pair of them sat there on the floor, gazing up, pulling rude faces and rocking from side to side with laughter.

The elevator stopped at the tenth floor while the woman, man and their dog alighted. As soon as they were out, Jerry pounded the "Close" button impatiently.

"Stop it, Wendy—I'm scared!" little Samantha gasped as she saw Wendy glaring at her, raising the knife slowly. She was almost in tears. Her fear was instantly communicated to Jason and he, too, began to whimper and back away frightened. Wendy moved forward, forcing them into a corner. Her jet-black, staring, expressionless eyes were by now bulging from their sockets.

Outside, Jerry sprinted down the corridor from the elevator. He was about to hammer on the door with his fist, then managed to compose himself and reached out and pressed the bell. There was no reply. He rapped on the door with his knuckles. Still no answer.

Then he leaned his ear against the wooden paneling of the door and listened. He could hear the frightened cries of the two children. Frantically, he beat on the door with his fist but, realizing it was not going to do any good, he fumbled hurriedly in his wallet and drew out a plastic credit card. Carefully, he wedged the edge of the card between the door and the jamb and slid it up and down until it came up against the flange of the lock. He pushed it firmly further into the narrow gap and the lock was pushed back, springing the door open.

As he barged breathlessly into the living room he was horrified to see the figure of Wendy, now totally bald, her face in a terrifying grimace of madness, the long carving knife poised high in the air above the heads of the two cowering children.

"No!" he shouted and Wendy whirled suddenly and charged at him. Jerry darted into the kitchen, then on into the dining room, overturning chairs behind him to try to block Wendy's path. The shrieking voices of the two children still rang out hysterically from the living room.

Wendy was backing him into a corner. She swung the knife in a wide arc and the blade slashed his arm. He quickly grabbed at her wrist before she could try again. But she seemed to have taken on superhuman strength and she wrenched her hand to one side, sending Jerry off-balance, crashing into a sliding glass door that opened out onto a small balcony. Jerry hit the concrete floor of the balcony amid a shower of broken glass and Wendy followed him out through the large hole that his body had made. He backed up into a corner of the balcony, bracing his body against the waist-high iron rail. Below lay a twenty-story drop to solid concrete. As Wendy lunged towards him, Jerry kicked out both his feet with all his might against her stomach. Wendy gasped, dropped the knife and staggered backwards. Off-balance, her feet flailing beneath her, Wendy hit the edge of the balcony rail with the small of her back and flipped backwards over the top. Without a sound, she plunged the 220 feet to her death on the asphalt below.

Slowly, Jerry moved forward, holding his badly-gashed arm away from his body. He moved to the front of the railing and leaned over, looking down. The broken figure of Wendy, one arm crushed beneath her in a grotesque position, lay crumpled and still on the asphalt, beside some children's swings in a small play area.

A bright patch of crimson was slowly spreading from beneath her head.

He bent down and picked up the carving knife from the

balcony floor, then stepped back into the apartment. Moving through the dining room, into the kitchen and then on to the hallway, he was startled to see the figure of Stephanie, squatting by the open front door, clutching the two sobbing children comfortingly to her breast. She looked up and her eyes widened in terror when she saw the bloody knife in Jerry's hand. Rising to her feet, she gasped.

"Where's Wendy? What did you do?" she demanded, horrified.

Then she lost her nerve. She put both hands up to her face and screamed hysterically, half-crying and half-laughing in shock.

Jerry dropped the knife and shot forward, placing his hand over Stephanie's mouth.

"Shut up!" he shouted as she struggled in his grasp, becoming even more hysterical. "Cut it out!"

The two children renewed their deafening wailing and he and Stephanie grappled in the open doorway. Jerry glanced down the hallway quickly and saw a man leaning out of one of the apartments, looking puzzled. He released his grip on Stephanie and darted down the corridor, past the man, toward the elevator. Stephanie's resumed shrieking echoed down the hallway.

"Help! Someone help!" she wailed. "Oh God! Please help!"

Jerry made it to the elevator and hit the ground floor button. The footsteps of the curious apartment dweller pounded on the carpeted floor as he gave chase. But before the man could reach the elevator and follow Jerry in, the doors closed. It seemed like an age before they opened again at street level.

Frantically, Jerry bounded out and ran across the spacious lobby reception area, past a completely surprised janitor and out into the street. Only a few blocks away from the apartment building, Jerry began to hear the approaching wail of police car sirens as he ran furtively along the streets, desperately trying to figure out where he could hide.

He ducked behind a parked truck as a police cruiser's head-lights stabbed through the growing twilight, rounding a corner ahead. He waited until the car was past, then, clutching his wounded arm that was still dripping blood on the sidewalk as he went along, he ran off into the darkness of an alley.

CHAPTER 18

"ED, THIS IS LIEUTENANT JENNINGS, HOMICIDE," Wayne Mulligan said, ushering the man of about mid-forties in a somewhat shabby trench coat into the campaign headquarters office. Edward Flemming reached out and took the newcomer's hand.

"I'm terribly sorry, Congressman," Jennings said, sympathetically. He knew that the boys from Homicide downtown had informed Flemming of his ex-wife's tragic death.

"Not yet," Flemming said, unemotionally. "I mean, I'm not Congressman yet. But thank you. Jennings?" He paused thoughtfully. "I don't recall—"

"Upstate," Jennings said. "Berkshire area. I'm covering a case that might have some bearing on your wife's death. The man I'm looking for fits the same description as her killer."

Flemming shot a glance at Wayne Mulligan. "Oh?" he said.

Jennings reached in an inside pocket and drew out a photograph.

"Remember him?" the detective said, handing it to Flemming.

Flemming studied the stock mugshot of a darkhaired young man; he was thin-featured with deeply-set, sad eyes and a symmetrical, strong jawline.

"Well, yes, I do," Flemming said. "Jerry...uh, Wayne, what did he say his name was?"

"Zipkin," Mulligan said, looking at the photograph. "Jerry Zipkin."

Jennings took the photograph back and put it in his pocket.

"The woman down the hall, a Stephanie—"

"Andretti," Flemming said.

"That's it," said Jennings. "She gave me the same name. I just like to be sure. He was with you at that rally in the shopping center. What were you talking about?"

Flemming glanced uneasily at Mulligan.

"Uh...I don't really recall," he said, scratching his forehead. "I just spoke to him very briefly...people come up to me all the time."

"He said he was looking for work," Mulligan said. "We didn't need anybody. But he wouldn't take no for an answer."

Lieutenant Jennings thought it strange that a man on the run from the police, wanted for the murder of three girls and a man, should be out in the open, job-hunting, looking for work with a prominent politician. But he did not say anything.

"That's when he approached me," Flemming said. "He asked me for a job, too. He got very pushy, grabbed my arm. Wayne here had to pull him away physically."

Jennings studied the ex-football player's muscular, burly figure.

"I'm sure you had no problem there," he said. Flemming and Mulligan smiled.

"Wayne's my walking insurance policy," he said.

"Well," Jennings said, blowing out his cheeks. "I guess that's it. We have a genuine maniac on our hands."

"What'd he do?" Flemming asked. "I mean upstate?"

"Oh, not much," Jennings said casually. "He just burned three girls in a fireplace and pushed his best friend in front of an eighteen-wheel truck."

Flemming shook his head, disgustedly. The detective went towards the door, then paused. He looked back at Flemming.

"You sure you didn't know Zipkin?"

Flemming shook his head.

"I told you. Only that one incident."

"He took an awful chance coming to you like that," Jennings said. "You sure all he said was he was looking for work?"

Flemming glanced at Mulligan who nodded his confirmation.

"I guess that makes him more of a maniac," Flemming said.

Jennings thought for a moment and seemed like he was about to speak. Then he shrugged and turned to go.

"I guess it does," he said. "You know, you try to make sense out of something that's so senseless."

"Sure, I know what you mean," said Flemming, relieved that the detective seemed satisfied and was not going to ask any more probing questions.

Jennings nodded in turn at Flemming and his right-hand-man and left.

There was still a trace of the February chill in the air, but weak, yellowy sunlight was filtering through and it had brought out a few early visitors to Central Park. There were men walking their dogs, the odd cyclist wheeling about the gravel tracks, the occasional hippie loafing on a bench, policemen on horseback, casually patrolling. And Jerry Zipkin.

Jerry sat hunched on a low wall beside a grassy knoll, his knees almost up to his chin. He had taken off his coat and draped it about him like a cape. Beneath the folds, he clutched at his wounded arm, out of sight of any curious passers-by.

Lost in his thoughts, his unshaven, weary face half-hidden behind his upturned collar, Jerry barely noticed as a scruffy, soiled and pale-faced youth strolled by. The youngster, his face haggard, drawn and blotchy, halted and stared at Jerry, as if he were a kindred spirit. Jerry looked up. The kid was obviously a junkie, looking to score.

"Hey, Jimmy," the junkie said, displaying a row of uneven, blackened teeth as he grinned stupidly. "How you been?"

Jerry straightened up and winced as the pain from his knife-wound played him up.

"You can't fight that feeling," the junkie said, mistaking Jerry's grimace for the hungry pangs of a dope habit. He ambled closer and put his face up close to Jerry's.

The kid's eyes were half-closed and haunted looking. His breath and body odor combined in a particularly repulsive bouquet.

"Say, Jimmy-boy," the junkie said, still grinning stupidly, his mouth hanging open. "Spot me a cigarette?"

Anxious to get rid of the intruder, Jerry reached in his pocket and brought out his cigarettes. The pair of them lit up, but the junkie showed no signs of leaving. A woman walked by, two children holding her hands. The children held back, staring quite openly at the two disheveled figures sitting near the grassy bank. The woman quickly pulled them away.

Next came an old, bald-headed man, walking his dog. He paused nearby, pulled out a handkerchief and mopped the perspiration from his brow. Jerry looked up, reminded of the bald, staring faces of Frannie Scott and Wendy Flemming and shuddered at the horror that the memory brought with it. The junkie, somehow sensing Jerry's revulsion, picked up the same feeling and began gibbering at the old man.

"G'wan, beat it!" he said, his junkie's paranoia growing all the time. "What the hell ya starin' at?"

The old man, startled and somewhat frightened by the sudden, unwarranted outburst, stuffed his handkerchief in his pocket and hurried away. By now the junkie was almost in a state of delirium, muttering and half-sobbing softly into the filthy collar of his shirt and holding onto Jerry's arm. He was badly in need of a fix, his nose running and his eyes all rheumy and watering. He raised his head and stared blankly across the park for a moment. Then suddenly he broke into a grin.

"There he is!" he said, excitedly, nudging Jerry. "Sweet Jesus hisself!"

Jerry followed the line of the junkie's gaze but could see only a few children playing football on the grass and a few odd strollers. The junkie was rummaging through the torn pockets of his jacket and jeans frantically. He eventually fumbled out a few tattered and crumpled dollar bills, his hands shaking terribly.

"Do it for me, Jimmy," he said, thrusting the money at Jerry. "You go talk to Jesus for us."

Jerry looked again in the direction the junkie was staring. A man was standing by a tree, the collar of his overcoat turned up. The junkie obviously thought it was his Man, his connection. But Jerry knew differently. Still clutching the junkie's tacky money, he got up and started away over the grass towards the silently waiting figure. Behind him he could hear the junkie giggling and babbling to himself in excited anticipation.

Within a few seconds, Jerry was within paces of the over-coated figure. The man's back was turned to him.

"Davie?" he said.

Dr. David Blume turned and cast an eye over Jerry and his grubby, disheveled condition.

"Jerry! What the hell happened to you?"

Self-consciously, Jerry ineffectively brushed at his coat and swept a hand through his hair.

"Where the hell have you been?" Blume said. "I've been standing here for about an hour, freezing my ass off!"

Jerry glanced cautiously around in the direction of the junkie. He was still sitting there, a pathetic, hunched figure, his hands clutching his stomach.

"You got the stuff?" Jerry asked.

Blume nodded slowly. He slipped a hand in his coat pocket and, with a quick glance around, handed a small, white packet to Jerry. The junkie watched eagerly from his squatting position near the grass knoll. To him it looked like a classic transaction, a score.

Jerry quickly and furtively pocketed the package.

"I feel like a goddamned pusher," Blume said, glancing around nervously. Jerry grinned with a mischievous glint in his eye.

"You're a natural, Davie," he said. "You sure this stuff will work?"

"Why don't you go over to the zoo and test it out," Blume said. "There's enough paraldehyde there to paralyze an elephant."

Jerry shook Blume's hand.

"Hey, Jerry," Blume said with a look of concern. "This is it. I don't want to see you anymore. I heard your name on the news. They're saying some pretty nasty things."

"But Davie—"

"I know, I know," Blume said quickly. "You think I'd be sticking my neck out if I thought you really did those things?" He grasped Jerry's hand warmly.

"Thanks, Davie," Jerry said.

"Sure," Blume said. "Oh...about that acid." Jerry nodded.

"I looked through the school yearbook. There was one guy on the football team who always wanted acid. Wayne Mulligan."

Jerry thought for a moment, silently mouthing the name. His face tightened into a grim smile.

"Thanks," he said and turned away.

The junkie watched Jerry walking away from the black-overcoated figure, not understanding. He stood up, as if about to follow. The man in the overcoat was walking away, too, in the opposite direction. The junkie's dulled mind could not figure out what was going on. The guy in the overcoat was the one with the stuff, but the other one, the younger guy, had scored and was walking off with *his* drugs, the horse that *he'd* paid for.

But he couldn't decide which of them to follow. He shrugged and stuffed his hands into the pockets of his torn and frayed jeans, hunched his shoulders and slouched off along the path, confused, following neither of them. He wasn't even sure what the hell he was doing here in the Park, except that he knew he needed a fix. He set off toward the sound of the traffic with a hollow gnawing in his stomach.

CHAPTER 19

LIEUTENANT JENNINGS WAS SITTING on top of a desk, his jacket draped over the back of a chair, in a borrowed office at the downtown Precinct House. He was reading one of Edward Flemming's campaign leaflets when the telephone rang.

"Dennis Jennings," he said.

"Lieutenant Jennings? Alicia Sweeny."

"Yes, dear."

"I think I can prove to you that Zippy's innocent."

Jennings swung his feet to the floor and slid off the desktop.

"Who?"

"Jerry —"

"Listen, Alicia," Jennings said, exhaling impatiently. "If you'll just tell me where Jerry is hiding out—"

"I don't know,' Alicia said emphatically. "I've been trying to reach him, but I can't. That's why I need your help."

"Help with what?"

"I'm meeting this guy tonight at the rally for Edward Flemming," Alicia said. "If you could have him tested, I'm sure you'll understand what's been happening."

"What if this fella checks out okay?"

Alicia took a deep breath.

"Then I'll help you find Jerry," she said, at last.

"Now you're talking, honey," Jennings said.

"Okay, where do I go?"

Alicia told him the details of the rally at Shopper's World and Jennings made notes on his blotter.

The salesman at Herman's Sporting Goods store took the handgun from the glass case behind the counter and held it out.

"Smith and Wesson," he said. "One-seventy-seven caliber, single action, loads one pellet at a time."

Jerry took the gun and examined it.

"Most powerful and accurate one in the store," the salesman said. "Thirty-nine-ninety-nine, plus tax."

Jerry hefted the gun in his palm, feeling the weight, checking its balance.

"Does this shoot target darts, too?" he asked.

"Sure does."

From a drawer behind the counter, the salesman took out a box of tiny, steel-tipped darts with feather flights. He shook one into his hand, took the gun from Jerry, inserted the dart into the loading chamber and handed back the weapon. He pointed toward a wooden door at the far end of the counter about fifteen feet away. Jerry shook his head, smiling, and handed the gun back.

The salesman took it, aimed at the door and squeezed the trigger. The gun made a dull report and Jerry looked toward the door to see the dart firmly embedded in the woodwork with only the feathers protruding.

"I'll take it," Jerry said. "Let me have a package of darts and a box of CO-2 cartridges."

While the salesman went for the darts and cartridges and began to make out a bill of sale, Jerry picked up the gun again and held it out at arm's length. A security guard by the front door of the store gave him a filthy look. Jerry was pointing the gun directly at him. Coloring, embarrassed, Jerry lowered the gun and placed it back on the counter.

By the time he reached Edward Flemming's campaign headquarters, wheeling the jeep around all the backstreets he could find en route, Flemming and two of his assistants had climbed into the politician's hired black Cadillac and driven away. Jerry nosed the jeep into the curb around the side of the store-front HQ and cut the engine.

Inside, a team of campaign workers were busy packing away leaflets, sashes, lapel-buttons and other paraphernalia into boxes, ready to load them into the vans that would take them off to Shopper's World for the final, big night of Flemming's whole campaign. As Jerry quietly entered, he caught sight of one of the girl helpers leaning into a packing case, her short skirt revealing her blue silk, lace-trimmed panties. He stood watching for a moment until the blonde girl straightened up and turned.

"Hi," she said. "Can I help you?"

Jerry glanced away, embarrassed at being caught ogling her that way.

"Uh...yeah, yeah you can," he said quietly. "I'm looking for Wayne Mulligan. Big guy, lots of muscles."

"I know who he is," the girl said, making a face.

"But he hasn't been around today. Thank God. He had one of his headaches."

"Oh, I see," Jerry said thoughtfully.

"Are you his friend?"

"Me? Nah."

She glanced around, then moved closer to Jerry, lowering her voice.

"Well I can tell you something about Wayne Mulligan," she said.

"You can?"

"He's a perv."

"Yeah?"

"A sex-crazed maniac," the girl said. "You know what he did? He grabbed me right here."

She put a hand between her legs.

"And he wouldn't let go," she said. "Could you imagine doing that in front of hundreds of people?"

Jerry smiled.

"No... not hundreds of people," he said wickedly. But the girl either didn't get his implication or was not shocked by it.

"Well, I'm glad the election is tomorrow so I won't have to see him after tonight," she said.

"What's tonight?" Jerry asked.

"The rally at Shopper's World. It's the last one. If he tries anything, I'm gonna call the cops on him."

"Shopper's World?"

"It's the biggest indoor shopping mall," the blonde said. "He's a psycho nut. I can tell. Did you ever look into his eyes?"

Jerry shook his head.

"They don't blink," the girl said. "He's always staring. It's disgusting."

She turned and walked away. The girl was undoubtedly right about Mulligan, Jerry was thinking. But nonetheless, he couldn't help staring himself as he watched the trim, undulating contours of her behind, wiggling pertly from side to side as she moved away.

CHAPTER 20

THEY COULDN'T HAVE DREAMED up a better name than Shopper's World if they had tried. Consumers were what made the business world go round and the great, indoor shopping complex was a microcosm of that world, the biggest shop window on the whole planet. All that Mr. and Mrs. Consumer had to bring was themselves, their credit cards or checkbooks. The rest, including the climate and fun for the kids, was laid on.

The massive complex seemed to stretch for miles in all directions from the wide, central Mall, the main walkway on the ground floor level. Rows and rows of open-fronted shops and stalls formed a labyrinth of aisles that reached away beneath the colorful overhead lighting as far as the eye could see. Everything in the Yellow Pages had its counterpart here and there were even a few concessions that you wouldn't find in the commercial phone book.

To break up what might have become the monotony of such a vast, ordered, right-angled layout of mini-streets, lighted fountains were dotted at intersections and carefully landscaped garden and plant arrangements and art displays broke up the symmetry at strategic points along the centers of the walkways.

Some of the store displays were ultra-modern, their products bathed in gently shifting shades of filtered lights. Others were designed to look ultra-antique, like the fairy-light-framed old-fashioned-style Penny Arcade, its multi-hued, garish bulbs flashing out their message in timed sequences. And the soda-fountains with their polished chromium seltzer dispensers and whirring cotton candy machines.

Taped Muzak, light, bouncy and totally innocuous, filtered down from hidden speakers in the voluminous drapes of a false ceiling, and beneath, in the basement, a huge central heating/air conditioning plant ensured all-year-round climate-controlled shopping comfort. The overall effect was of a computer-planned, multi-million-dollar cross between a carnival midway and a super department store, circa 2000 A.D. Orwell would have hated it, but Marshall McLuhan would have WHOOOOOPED for joy at its multi-media ingenuity.

Edward Flemming was simply glad of the chance to take advantage of the terrific, surefire, crowd-pulling venture. Behind the bunting-draped speaking platform, out along the main Mall, Flemming was sitting inside his prefabricated, portable office, hunched over a desk, studying his speech for the big night. His aides were in a huddle in a corner, discussing last-minute arrangements, ticking off extensive checklists. Outside, where the other workers were making everything ready for Flemming's appearance, music boomed out from the string puppet show beside the campaign stand. It had been a great idea, booking in the puppet act. It was bound to draw in the kids and, along with them, their young, voting-age parents. The rows of folding chairs in front of the platform were already nearly full and Flemming's uniformed helpers were unstacking more as the crowd grew. If this wasn't the final clincher that would ensure Flemming's seat in Congress, it was doubtful if anything else ever would.

Flemming looked up from his desk.

"Wayne!" he called, looking at the informal confab in the corner. "Where the hell is Wayne?"

"I haven't seen him, Mr. Flemming," one of the aides, a youngish man holding a clipboard, answered.

"Don't tell me he has one of his famous headaches," Flemming said, angrily. "Try to find him."

"Yes, sir."

The young man went out.

Outside on the small puppet stage to one side of the speaking platform, a marionette doll caricature of Barbra Streisand was moving its jerky, segmented jaw, miming to the real Miss Streisand's record of *The Way We Were.*

The music, pumped out over a small amplifier system, was competing with the low, bass thump that echoed out from the Peachtrees discotheque some thirty yards away down the central Mall. Inside the disco a motley group of young people in the twenties-to-thirties bracket, were jerking like puppets themselves while a DJ shuffled records inside a turntable booth with mirrored walls. Strobes and liquid, moving oil-filter lights sent a kaleidoscope of color over the plushly-draped interior of the disco, the lights pulsating in time with the heavy beat of the music.

Beside the smoothly-polished, laminated dance floor was a long, fully-stocked bar. Wayne Mulligan was leaning against it, elbow on the bar top, his head propped in his hand. His drink lay untouched at his elbow and Wayne was wondering how much longer he would be able to tolerate the punishing volume of the music belting out from four large speakers set in each corner of the discotheque.

He picked up his drink and in one rapid movement drained the contents of the glass down his throat without even tasting the liquor. He put the glass down on the bar and raised both hands to his ears, trying to shut out the noise.

"Hi," Alicia said, suddenly appearing at his elbow. But Wayne did not hear. She touched his arm and he turned.

He tried to smile but as he lowered his hands from his ears, the music assaulted his brain again and the smile became more of a grimace.

"I think I'll have a drink," Alicia said. A bartender hovered in front of her. "Vodka martini, please."

The barman went off to fix her drink and she turned back to Wayne.

"How's it going?"

"What?" Wayne shouted, still screwing up his face at the volume of the music.

"The rally," Alicia said, raising her voice.

"Oh," Wayne said, lip-reading, rather than hearing what she had said. "I…haven't been feeling too well. I haven't been over there yet."

Alicia studied him. His face was tense and strained. He looked like he might crack up at any moment, like someone on the verge of a serious nervous breakdown. Not wanting him to see her concern, Alicia turned away, glancing around the room at the crowd, the men in waisted, light-tone suits, matching vests and flared trousers, the girls in bright, slinky cocktail-style ensembles, with plunging necklines, their bodies outlined against the material of their dresses as they shook and writhed on the dance floor. Where in hell was Lieutenant Jennings, she wondered.

"Who are you looking for? Wayne asked.

"No one," she said, turning back to him. "I've never been here before." She nodded toward the disco with its garish, over-done decor. "Nice, isn't it?" she said.

Wayne pulled a face.

"Music's too loud," he said, reaching up to loosen his tie. Beads of perspiration were standing out on his forehead and he looked as if he would never be able to acclimatize himself to the volume of the records.

"I'm going to wash up," he said. "Be right back."

Alicia was glad of the chance to think. What would she do, or even what *could* she do, if Wayne Mulligan came unstuck right here? She looked around as Wayne strode quickly away toward the Men's Room. There were plenty of people around. She'd probably be all right. Someone would be bound to come to her aid if Wayne started acting up. She wondered where Jerry was.

At that moment, Jerry was outside on the spacious parking lot, sitting in his jeep. By the light of a flashlight he was unwrapping the small phial of tranquilizer that Dr. Blume had given him. Next he took out one of the red-feathered darts and dipped the pointed tip in the liquid paraldehyde. From under his driver's seat he reached out the single-action Smith & Wesson. He inserted a CO-2 cartridge, then loaded the dart into the chamber. He was about to get out of the jeep when something occurred to him. As an added precaution, he took out another of the tiny darts, coated its tip in the paraldehyde and wrapped it in tinfoil, placing it carefully in his pocket.

He climbed out of the jeep and straightened up, preparing to put the gun in the pocket of his chinos. Then he saw the blue Chevy Monte Carlo draw up in front of the Shopping Center's main entrance. Quickly, Jerry dived back in his jeep and ducked down, lying across the front seats.

Lieutenant Dennis Jennings got out of his car and entered the shopping complex. The sound of music from the discotheque filtered out across the parking lot as the doors swung open to admit him.

Cautiously, Jerry peered over the door of his jeep, saw that the Monte Carlo was parked and empty outside the center, and climbed out onto the asphalt. He slid the gun into his pocket then began to walk briskly towards the brightly-lit precinct. On the way, he passed a phone booth and, on impulse, doubled back, went inside and dialed Alicia's home number. He stood there a few moments, listening to the ringing tone. Then he replaced the receiver, stepped out of the booth and walked toward the automatic, sliding glass double doors leading into Shopper's World.

Trying to look as inconspicuous as possible, Jerry strolled casually along the terrazzo floors of the center, glancing at the open frontages of the shops, but staying toward the middle of the aisles to be as far out of the lights as possible. As he walked, he looked down and was relieved to see that the handgun was not conspicuous in the pocket of his loosely-fitting trousers.

He had chosen the right-hand pocket because the bullet wound in his shoulder seemed to have stopped troubling him quite so much since Dr. Blume's rapid treatment. His other arm still ached a little from the knife wound. But he had not been able to risk trying to get that treated. Instead he had bought some antiseptic at a drugstore, soaked his handkerchief in it and bound it around the forearm, where Wendy Flemming's kitchen knife had left a three-inch gash. At least it had stopped the bleeding.

There was one consolation for looking so disheveled, unshaven and scruffy. None of the concession holders attempted to lure him into their shop displays; he didn't look like a shopper come to spend his money, more like a workman who had perhaps been helping to assemble some of the displays.

In any case, many of the stores were beginning to show signs of clearing up and closing. The main events of the evening were the disco and the Flemming rally.

At the far end of the central Mall, Jerry spotted the puppet show in progress beside Flemming's bunting-hung platform. Skirting around the edge of the seated audience, Jerry stood on the periphery of the scene in half-shadow. He leaned on a wall and watched the show while he figured out what he had come here to do tonight.

The Barbra Streisand puppet had come to the end of her act and was bowing by the side of the

miniature stage, before ducking behind the curtains. The tiny spotlights on the stage went down, leaving it in darkness, as the audience applauded and the children cheered. Then, an announcer's voice came over the loudspeakers.

"Ladies and Gentlemen," he said, "for the first time, live at Shopper's World...Ole Blue Eyes himself—Frank Sinatra!"

There was another burst of applause from the crowd and a mild gasp of approval as an extremely cleverly made puppet caricature of Sinatra stepped into center-stage and the spotlight went up. The puppet, decked out in a midnight blue tuxedo and bowtie, gave a curt, Sinatra-ish bow.

Alicia was finishing her third vodka martini at the discotheque bar and starting to wonder if Wayne Mulligan had deserted her. She was beginning to feel a little high, standing there alone with no one to talk to and the thumping disco music still pounding away. Maybe, she thought, maybe he's gone off to report to Flemming at the rally. And she was considering going off to find him when she spotted Lieutenant Jennings shouldering his way through the dancers and looking around anxiously. Alicia stood on tiptoe and raised a hand, waving to him. Jennings caught sight of her and she beckoned him over.

Easing his way through the crowds, Jennings came up, flashing a smile of greeting. He looked up and down the bar, then at Alicia.

"Which one is he? he said, putting his face close to her ear so that he would not have to shout too loud to be heard.

She shook her head.

"He's not here," she said. "He said he was going to the Men's Room. It's been about twenty minutes. I don't know what happened to him."

There was a faint, almost hysterical note of anxiety in her

voice, her words tripping out rapidly and Jennings looked in her face and noticed that her eyes were slightly glassy.

"I'll go check," he said, eyeing the drink in her hand. "Are you okay?"

"Just fine," Alicia said.

"Stay here," he said. "I'll go check."

He was about to turn and leave, then paused. "What's his name?"

"Mulligan. Wayne Mulligan."

Alicia smiled tipsily as Jennings fought his way out across the dance floor. The DJ had slapped on a Reggae disc and Jennings had to weave and duck awkwardly through the forest of flailing arms and out-thrust elbows of the dancers.

Wayne Mulligan was standing over the washbasin in the Men's Room, his head ducked down into a sinkful of cold water. He had put in the plug and left the tap running and the water was brimming over the edge of the bowl and onto the floor. A young man saw him standing there, hunched, immobile, and went over.

"Hey, buddy, you okay? he said.

The figure leaning into the sink basin did not move. The front of his hair was sopping wet and plastered to his forehead.

Just then, Jennings entered.

The young man looked at the newcomer.

"This your friend?" he asked. "I think he drank too much."

Jennings quickly sized up the situation and moved in front of the young man.

"Okay, son," he said. "I'll take care of it."

"He was like that when I came in," the young man said. "Better get him some air."

He glanced again at the figure of Wayne, then went out. Jennings reached over and turned off the water tap.

"Okay, Wayne," he said, grasping the ex-footballer by the waist and pulling him away from the basin. "Upsy-daisy!"

As the detective got Mulligan upright, he loosened his hold. Then without warning, Mulligan lashed out backwards violently with both elbows, then swung around. The vicious, stabbing blows and the violent swing sent Jennings staggering backwards across the washroom until his head crashed into the solid, tiled wall. Stunned, his head ringing from the blow, Jennings leaned back against the wall, looking vaguely at Mulligan. Jennings' face was frozen in a peculiar expression, half surprised, half afraid.

Mulligan's eyes were staring horribly at him and seemed to be black, empty pits of animal hatred. His matted, dripping wet hair was plastered down his forehead in grotesque fingers, making him look like some latter-day creation of Baron Frankenstein.

Before Jennings could recover himself, Mulligan shot out a huge hand and grabbed a fistful of coat and shirt-collar. Then, shaking him like a rag doll, he slammed the detective's head violently against the hard wall again and again, the back of his skull making dull, sickening thuds. Almost detachedly, as if it were happening to someone else, Jennings was listening to the sounds, counting the blows vaguely and watching the strange red mist permeate his vision. Then...blackness.

Mulligan stepped back, letting go of the detective's throat, and watched, unemotionally, as the battered figure slumped to the floor, sliding down the wall and leaving a wide, bloody smear, like the tail of a fiery comet streaked up the tiles behind him.

Then Mulligan whirled and caught sight of himself in the mirror on the opposite wall. He snarled like an animal, saliva dribbling from his twisted mouth, reached up and tore the drenched wig from his bald head. Glaring at the hideous, grimacing, hollow-eyed ghoul confronting him, Wayne clawed at the mirror, as if trying to strangle his own reflection, his rage increasing as his fingertips slid ineffectively down the glass.

With a terrible, agonized roar, he hauled back, then slammed his huge, clenched fist forward, smashing the mirror to pieces. And as the razor-sharp shards of glass fell to the floor, he brought his big-booted foot down upon them, stomping them insanely, as if trying to erase forever the image he had seen there.

CHAPTER 21

THE DISCO WAS an uproar of whirling and twisting bodies, the dance floor crammed solid, as the music tempo grew faster and the volume from the quadrophonic sound system was pumped up even louder by the DJ in his turntable booth. It was even worse, a few seconds later, when Wayne Mulligan put in an unannounced appearance.

Wayne staggered in blindly, not realizing where he was going or what he was doing. The hellish turmoil taking place inside his head was almost crippling. The loud noise of the disco music didn't help. In fact, it made his torment even more unbearable. He stumbled, barreling into people at the edge of the dance floor and reached up, cramming his hands over his ears to try to block out the deafening cacophony. But it was no good. He was completely unhinged.

He grabbed one of the leather chairs beside a table at the edge of the floor and hurled it into a speaker mounted high in the corner. Then he crashed his way through to the center of the dancers and grabbed a cavorting little blonde around the waist from behind, whirling her around. At first, she laughed, thinking it was some guy she'd been dancing with earlier, but her expression changed suddenly to one of breathtaking bewilderment when she felt herself being lifted bodily, high in the air.

For a second or two she felt herself whirled around dizzily as Mulligan held her up above his head like a wrestler, the lights and colors of the disco whizzing crazily in a spiral. Then he flung her right across the room, over the heads of the scattering dancers, and she landed painfully, her back across a table full of drinks where a bunch of people were sitting. Several girls screamed.

A stocky young man in the crowd nearest to Wayne, horrified at what he had just seen, stepped forward, drew back his arm and launched a solid straight jab at the jaw of the husky, bald-headed figure. With anyone else, the punch would probably have laid him low. The only effect it had on Wayne was to enrage him even more.

He lashed out savagely, his arms shooting back and forth like high-speed piledrivers, and the young Galahad went down under the hail of devastating blows to his head and body.

The crowd backed away, panicking at the sight of the giant, bald-headed madman with the staring black eyes, pushing and banging into each other as they tried to keep out of his reach. Several people fell over in the crush and more girls began to shriek and scream in terror.

At the far end of the dance floor, the DJ saw the commotion and took off his headphones, staring disbelievingly at the scene before him.

Over by the bar, Alicia heard the screams and saw the sea of bobbing heads and the struggling mass of people, but she could not see exactly what was going on. She began to fight her way through the jostling crowd at the edge of the dance floor to see what was happening.

Outside, down the Mall, the puppet-Sinatra was telling everybody how he'd done it his way. To Jerry Zipkin, the harsh lines and angles of the caricature Sinatra, with its exaggerated mannerisms and features, was not amusing. It was disturbing. Especially singing *My Way* ...

It took Jerry back to a night only a week ago when he had watched his friend Frannie Scott standing under the improvised spot of a table lamp, Sinatra, singing exactly that song. And that had been the start of it all.

The pretty, blonde-haired campaign worker that Jerry had met down at Flemming's headquarters came wiggling by, carrying a soft drink and heading for the speaking platform. She smiled as she recognized Jerry. It snapped him out of his distasteful, macabre remembrances of the past week or so.

"Hey," he called. "When you go up there can you tell Wayne Mulligan to come out? I want to talk to him?"

"I haven't seen him," the girl said.

Jerry frowned. The girl waved the drink she was carrying.

"Excuse me," she said. "I'd better get this to Mr. Flemming."

She turned and moved off toward the rear of the speaking podium. Halfway there, a uniformed security guard dashed out of the shadows from behind the platform and bumped into her, almost spilling the drink she was carrying. Without pausing to apologize, the man dashed off down the Mall and went into the discotheque.

Jerry looked after him, puzzled, just as the crowd applauded at the end of the Sinatra-puppet's number.

"And now," the puppet was saying, "the real star of the show. Let's have a big hand for our next Congressman—Edward Flemming!"

The applause rose again as the spotlight switched to the center of the podium and Edward Flemming stepped into it, smiling his dazzlingly disarming politician's smile.

The crowd in the disco had formed a wide circle, backing away, leaving the deranged Wayne Mulligan standing in the center of the dance floor, looking around him wildly. Two hefty bouncers shouldered their way through the onlookers from opposite directions. One of them carried a large wooden club, like a patrolman's night-stick.

"Easy fella," one of the bouncers yelled, edging forward, trying to keep Wayne's attention while his partner moved in from behind with the club. "Nobody's gonna hurt ya."

The man with the club rushed up behind Wayne, raising the weapon to strike. But Wayne lashed forward at the first man, ripping great gouges of flesh from his face with his fingernails, like some wild beast. The man screamed in pain, throwing up his arms to his torn face, and the other brought down the club savagely on the back of Wayne's head. But it did not seem to have any effect. While his partner sank to the floor, still clutching his gashed face, the club-wielding bouncer leaped on Wayne's back, trying to grasp him around the neck.

Wayne took hold of the man's legs and swung him around and around like a doll. The momentum made him lose his grip and, like a display ice skater, he was whirled around and around, his arms thrown out above his head. Then Wayne let go.

The bouncer sailed several feet through the air and crashed down in the back of the booth where the DJ crouched, horrified. The mirrors set into the rear walls of the booth quivered briefly, then shattered into a thousand pieces.

Just then the uniformed security guard pushed his way to the edge of the crowd by the Mall entrance. He drew out his service revolver and aimed it at Wayne, steadying his right wrist with his left hand, just like in the movies.

"Okay. Hold it!" he shouted.

Alicia was standing by the guard's elbow. She realized, tipsy as she was, that if the man shot Wayne it would be Jerry's last chance of proving his innocence. Mulligan had to be stopped, alive, so that proper tests could be made.

She grabbed the guard's arm.

"No! Don't!" she cried.

The man's arm came down, the gun went off and a bullet sank into the polished floorboards.

The loud report acted like a signal to the disco crowd. In one mad, panic-stricken rush, everyone bolted for the doors. Before the guard could get off another shot Mulligan was upon him, smashing him to the floor in a terrible barrage of blows. Then, Alicia found herself confronted by the madman with super-human strength.

For a moment, Wayne stood looking at her, confusedly. She stood paralyzed, too afraid even to back away, in case he lunged out and grabbed her.

The DJ, having seen the effect that the music seemed to have on the maniac intruder, suddenly boosted the volume up to full blast. With a terrible scream of anguish, Wayne whirled, hands to his ears, ran across the dance floor and crashed out a door in the back of the disco.

Alicia was standing there, still frozen to the spot, when she saw Lieutenant Jennings, stumbling in from the Men's Room, clutching the back of his head.

CHAPTER 22

Edward Flemming was halfway through his speech when the crowd of young people burst out of the discotheque and came streaming up the Mall panic-stricken, as if the place were on fire. He began to falter as he saw them rushing by, white-faced, some of the men supporting their girlfriends who were sobbing and wailing. It was while he was trying to figure out what the strange, noisy exodus could mean, that he spotted Jerry Zipkin at the rear of his audience. Zipkin, the guy the cops were looking for; the guy that murdered Wendy and threatened her neighbor and kids with a kitchen knife. The man who murdered Frannie Scott and was trying to blow his career sky high with some crap about LSD at college ten years ago.

It was at that moment that Flemming gave up on his speech entirely. Without even excusing himself, he bounded down off the platform and headed towards the rear of the audience.

Just then, Jerry had grabbed the arm of one of the young men streaming past in the crowd. "Hey, what happened?" Jerry said.

"There's a bald-headed maniac in there," the man said, breathlessly, pointing back at the disco. "He's really berserk!"

The kid broke free and moved on. Jerry looked down the Mall towards the Peachtrees. He could hear the music blasting out of the place and the wailing and cries of the crowd still streaming out. Then a hand grabbed his arm and another his neck and he was staring into the face of Edward Flemming.

"You dirty bastard!" Flemming spat.

"Leggo of me!" Jerry said, squirming in Flemming's grip. "I didn't kill anybody!"

"Like hell you didn't!" Flemming said. He turned and called back over his shoulder towards the platform. "Hey, Wayne! Get me Wayne!"

Jerry reached out and shook Flemming by the shoulders so that he turned to face him again.

"Your campaign manager's in that club over there, ripping the joint apart," he said. "He took some of that acid you sold. So did your wife."

Flemming blanched and stared in utter shock at Jerry's words. He released his hold a little and Jerry squirmed free and ran off towards the discotheque, leaving the politician standing there, awestricken.

Jerry crept warily into the disco. The music was so deafening it was painful. He moved cautiously further into the place and looked around. The place was deserted, apart from one or two unconscious bodies lying dotted about the floor.

"Zippy!"

He looked across the far corner and there was Alicia. Jerry ran over and saw that she was holding a wet handkerchief on the back of Lieutenant Jennings' bloody head. The detective was stretched out on a leather couch in a corner of the room.

"What are you doing here?" Jerry shouted, trying to compete with the noise.

"I was trying to help you," Alicia yelled. "This is Lieutenant Jennings."

Jerry looked down at the injured man on the couch. He began to proffer his hand but saw quickly that the cop was in no shape for such formalities. He was glassy-eyed, like a man who had only just recovered consciousness and wasn't really sure whether he could hold on to it. Jerry glanced around the place. Tables and chairs were scattered and upended and there was broken glass everywhere. A girl lay moaning beneath an upturned table and the still form of the uniformed security man lay at the edge of the dance floor.

"Where is he?" Jerry yelled.

Alicia couldn't hear. She mimed the fact, pointing at her ear, then at one of the speakers behind him. Jerry looked up and saw that it had been smashed in, but was still working.

He ran across the dance floor to the turntable booth. The DJ was sitting there staring, in shock, still only half believing what he had seen.

Jerry made a quick sign to him to turn down the music. The DJ just stared.

"Shut it!" Jerry screamed, pointing at the turntable.

The DJ continued to sit there, staring uncomprehendingly.

Jerry pulled out his Smith & Wesson and waved it in the DJ's face.

"Shut it!" he yelled again. The DJ shut it.

The silence hit the place like a sledgehammer. Jerry's and Alicia's and Jennings' ears rang with the after-effects of the music in the sudden, utter stillness. Alicia's especially. After all the vodka martinis, the panic, the fear and the violence, she was feeling quite drunk. As Jerry returned she whirled a little too quickly and almost fell over. He caught her.

"Need honey?" he said.

She nodded stupidly. "Where's Wayne?"

Alicia pointed towards the back exit. Jerry pulled out the gun again and ran off.

"Zippy!" Alicia called. "Be careful!" He went out.

Systematically, Jerry walked from one side of the ground-floor complex to the other, peering down each of the aisles. Then he crossed back again at the halfway intersection and looked down each one again. All he saw were concession holders closing up their stands and a few late stragglers wending their way to the main exit. Nor was there a sound from any of the closed-down stalls. It could mean one of two possibilities. Either Wayne was hiding, laying low in one of the darkened booths, waiting for everyone to leave. Or he had gone up to the department store proper on the first floor of the Shopper's World complex.

The first alternative did not seem terribly likely. From what Jerry had seen and heard, Wayne was not acting with furtive cunning, like the ordinary psycho. He had been blundering about, attacking people indiscriminately and noisily. So, he had to be up on the first floor. Jerry headed off towards the escalator.

Mrs. Elaine Delacourt, manageress of the first-floor jewelry department, never knew how lucky she was that night. She was putting away the rings and bracelets and necklaces from their display cases and placing them in velvet-lined trays in the lock-up drawers beneath the counters. And she was cursing quietly the tangled-up necklace that she was holding. It probably saved her life.

While she was untangling it, Wayne Mulligan was just entering the store. The lights were still on and the doors were unlocked and here and there employees were going about their closing-up rituals. The time it took Wayne to make his way through the store into the jewelry department was the time it took Mrs. Delacourt to untangle the necklace. And, just as he approached the counter where she was at work, Mrs. Delacourt ducked down, to put the necklace away. Wayne walked by, peering around him and, because she was beneath the level of the counter-top, he didn't see her and walked right on by.

Jerry Zipkin wandered through the store, the Smith & Wesson in his trouser pocket, looking around nervously as he passed through the various departments: Hardware, Carpeting, Ladies' Lingerie.

It was just as he rounded the corner into the Junior Miss Department that he caught a glimpse of a bald head up in front. His heart pounding, Jerry silently ducked behind one of the displays. He slipped the gun from his pocket, still loaded with the powerful, tranquillizer-soaked dart, and began to creep forward, crouching low so that he would be obscured by the counters and displays between himself and Mulligan. Closer and closer he got, until he was sure he could hit his target.

The figure had not moved. It stood there, black-eyed and staring, as if listening for something.

Jerry took a deep breath and began to raise the gun. It was only when he took careful aim that he saw his mistake. The bald figure was nothing more than a store mannequin, stripped of its clothes and wig, ready for the dressers to go to work the following morning before the store re-opened. For the first time in his life, Jerry found department store Muzak, which was still playing, curiously soothing. When he looked around he saw that there were lots more of the naked, bald mannequins about the store. He straightened up, looking warily in all directions, then moved on.

It was in the Record Department that Jerry finally caught up with Wayne.

Heavy rock music was pounding out from a stereo as Harry Parton, the young department manager fiddled with the cash register tabulator, adding up the day's takings on a pocket calculator. His assistant, Jayne Harley, was busy picking up stacks of records and replacing them in the empty holders on the wire racks down the center of the floor area opposite the counter. She was about to slide a handful of albums into a space on one of the racks when she saw, peering at her through the common space between the holders, a hideous, dour-white face with black, malignant eyes. Jayne got ready to scream, but before she could, the whole rack came crashing down on top of her.

Harry looked up from the cash register and saw the bizarre, frightening figure of Wayne Mulligan, lurching towards him. He grabbed a broom that was leaning in the corner and vaulted the counter to confront the menacing weirdo. He thrust out the broom handle to fend off this staring, nightmarish creature, but Mulligan grabbed it and snatched it from his hands. Then he picked young Harry up and hurled him backwards through the air, arms and legs flailing, until he fell into another rack of records.

Just then, Jerry appeared in the archway leading from the Electrical Appliances Department. "Wayne!" he screamed.

As Wayne turned, Jerry picked up a clock-radio from a nearby counter and threw it at him. The flying object, which struck Wayne on the shoulder and bounced off, diverted the maniac's attention from the poor young guy lying half-buried beneath a pile of 12-inch records and sleeves.

But it alerted his attention to Jerry. Wayne growled like a wildcat and came at him.

There was no time to raise and aim the gun. Jerry turned on his heels and ran. As he darted from department to department, dodging down side-aisles, Jerry felt the strange, cold, tinglingly electric sensation of fear and panic running through his body. It was a feeling he hadn't had since he was a kid; the self-induced terror when the one being chased senses his pursuer right behind him.

Suddenly, Jerry's foot snagged on the jutting corner-beading of one of the counters and he pitched forwards, headlong. He rolled over onto his back, struggling frantically to tug out the gun and looked up with a momentary gasp of horror when he saw a whole crowd of white-faced, black-eyed figures with terribly obvious wigs, surrounding him. He had fallen into a cluster of store mannequins.

Beyond them, Wayne was only a few paces away, hurtling towards him like an enraged bull. Jerry raised the pistol, aimed and, at the last moment, squeezed the trigger. Wayne halted suddenly in his tracks, his hands going up involuntarily to his neck, where the little, red-feathered dart was embedded. He reeled, staggering around for a moment, then his fingers found the dart and he tore it free, hurling it away from him angrily. He reached down, grabbed Jerry like a toy and flung him sprawling along one of the aisles.

On his hands and knees, bruised and painfully lacerated, Jerry scrambled frantically forward and ducked into the narrow opening between the counters. He heard Wayne's footsteps and heavy, labored breathing coming closer as he reached in his pocket for the tiny roll of tinfoil containing the other paraldehyde-coated dart. His only one.

Fumbling desperately, he unwrapped the foil and quickly crammed the dart into the chamber. Then he crawled stealthily forward, listening for noises that would tell him of Wayne's whereabouts. He peered out cautiously from between the counters, then scrambled across the aisle behind another counter. He could hear Wayne's footsteps and half-animal grunts somewhere ahead.

Slowly, Jerry rose to a standing position, the gun raised before him. He took a long deep breath, trying not to make the slightest sound as he gripped the weapon with both hands to Steady it. He held his breath. Wayne was straight ahead, his back towards Jerry.

Jerry took aim and fired. The dart struck dead center, between Wayne's shoulder blades. With a wild roar, Wayne reached behind him, trying to tear the dart out of his body, as he had done the first one. But he could not reach it. He half-turned, as if to come to Jerry again, but suddenly he stiffened in his tracks, his whole body quivering, his eyes bulging. Then he pitched forward, crashing through a display stand and sprawled full-length on a section of marble flooring.

Warily, Jerry came out from behind the counter, still holding the gun in front of him, even though it was no longer of any use. The rest of the pellets were back in the jeep. He stood over Wayne and looked down. One of Wayne's legs twitched in an involuntary spasm, momentarily, from the effects of the drug. Then he was still. The big, ex-football player was helpless. He lay there, his black eyes staring wide, but glazed over. His breath was coming in painful, heaving gasps.

Jerry knelt down and lifted Wayne's head into his lap. And suddenly, he felt sorry for this giant of a man who had run amok, mindlessly smashing people and objects aside like matchsticks, who had almost killed a Homicide detective by beating his head in against a wall. Sorry because now, as Wayne lay helpless and immobile, a pitiful sight with his large, white, domed head, Jerry realized that Wayne and Frannie and Wendy Flemming and John O'Malley had only made one simple, awful mistake in the whole of their lives. All they had done, ten years ago, when life was mad and reckless and uncertain, was dropped a tab of bad acid. A strain of LSD that, over the years, had destroyed their reason and brought them to their tragic predicaments.

And Jerry put his head down, resting it on Wayne's chest, and wept. For all of them.

EPILOGUE

LIEUTENANT DENNIS JENNINGS was sitting up in bed with his head swathed in bandages. Dr. Blume entered the ward and came over to his bedside.

"How's the head feeling, Lieutenant?" Jennings smiled wryly.

"I'll live," he said. "What about Mulligan?"

Dr. Blume drew in a breath through clenched teeth and looked pensively out of the window.

"We still can't be sure," he said. "But preliminary tests of the white blood cells show massive chromosomal aberration."

The detective shook his head sadly in reflection. "Blue Sunshine?"

The surgeon did not answer. He was still staring off into space, lost in some private train of thought. Then he turned and, with only a brief glance at Jennings, went off towards the door.

"Hey, Doc," Jennings called, "how long before I can ski?"

"Give it a couple of weeks," Dr. Blume said, pausing by the door.

"Doc, if you see Zipkin, tell him I'm sorry. The poor kid must've been through hell."

Dr. Blume nodded his understanding. "I will," he said and went out.

Alicia was sitting on the long leather couch in Dr. Blume's office. For once, her natural good looks were tarnished by the strain and weariness in her face. She had not slept since the mayhem of the previous night at the discotheque. Now, as pale, late February sunlight filtered down through the window, she sat there, slowly spooning honey into her mouth from a jar.

Jerry was leaning on the opposite wall beside the window. He was totally exhausted, too, but for the moment was still refusing to give in to it. It was only the peculiar, vague feeling of half-reality that he was experiencing after his long ordeal, that was keeping him conscious. He glanced across at Alicia, eating the honey, and had to look away, nauseated at the thought of the sweet, sticky, undiluted syrup.

Edward Flemming stood silently by the door in his smartly-tailored grey suit, not looking at anyone or anything in particular.

The door opened and Dr. Blume came in. "How's Wayne?" Flemming asked.

Blume shrugged, noncommittally.

"Too early to tell," he said. "That tranquilizer is still working."

Flemming paced nervously across the room and turned. Then he thumped the desk-top with his fist.

"Damn it!" he said, angrily. "I should have known what the hell that stuff was."

Jerry looked at him from beneath half-closed eyelids.

"Nobody knew what they were taking in those days," he said quietly. "They just took a chance."

"He's right," Dr. Blume said. Alicia glanced at her watch.

"Hey—it's election day," she said, looking at Flemming "Don't you have to vote?"

Flemming looked at her dejectedly.

"What for?" he said. He reached out and picked up the morning newspaper from the Doctor's desk, then slammed it sharply down again. The front page was almost entirely devoted to the story of the uproar at Shopper's World the night before.

"I don't have a chance," Flemming said.

He stared silently out the window for a moment, then turned towards the place where Jerry had been leaning on the wall. But Jerry was no longer there. While Flemming's back was turned, Jerry had gone into the examining room and was lying down on the low couch there. Seeing Flemming looking around, confused, Alicia got up, peeped into the anteroom and smiled, signaling to Flemming where Jerry was.

Then she pulled the door quietly, leaving it only slightly ajar.

"Alicia's right," Dr. Blume told Flemming. "You'd better go vote. At least we know that this is over."

Flemming frowned and looked at him. "Is it?"

Dr. Blume raised a quizzical eyebrow.

"You said that you only had four tabs of Blue Sunshine."

Flemming turned back to gaze out the window.

"That's right," he said. "But you realize I didn't make the stuff. I just dealt. The guy I bought it from had hundreds of tabs…"

On the examination room table, Jerry Zipkin's eyes suddenly flickered open. He had heard what Flemming was saying. Every word had filtered through.

"The guy was from California," Flemming went on. "I never knew his name…"

Exhausted as he was, Jerry knew at that moment that he was not going to get his much-needed sleep. Not for a long, long time. And that went for Dr. Blume and Flemming too. Blue Sunshine raised a great number of questions, and they were the only people who knew any of the answers…

The following pages include various poster art used in the promotion of Blue Sunshine across the world as well as images from the film. Used by permission.

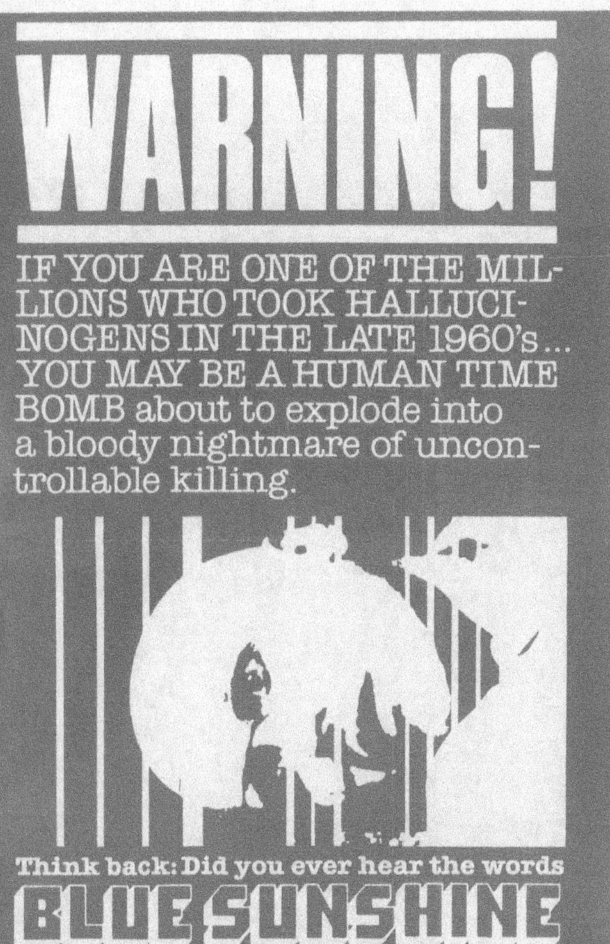

BLUE
SUNSHINE

BLUE SUNSHINE

A Special Task Force for the United States
Federal Drug Administration reports that
two hundred and fifty-five doses of
"BLUE SUNSHINE" manufactured in
September 1967 are still unaccounted for.

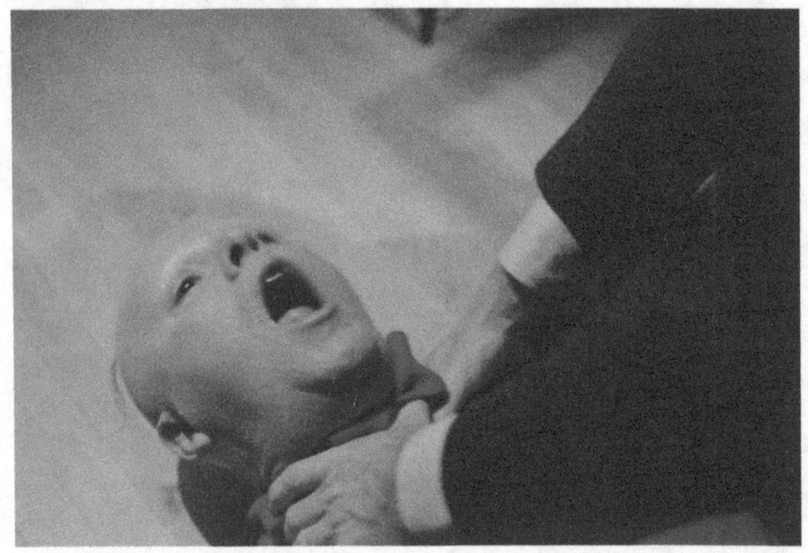

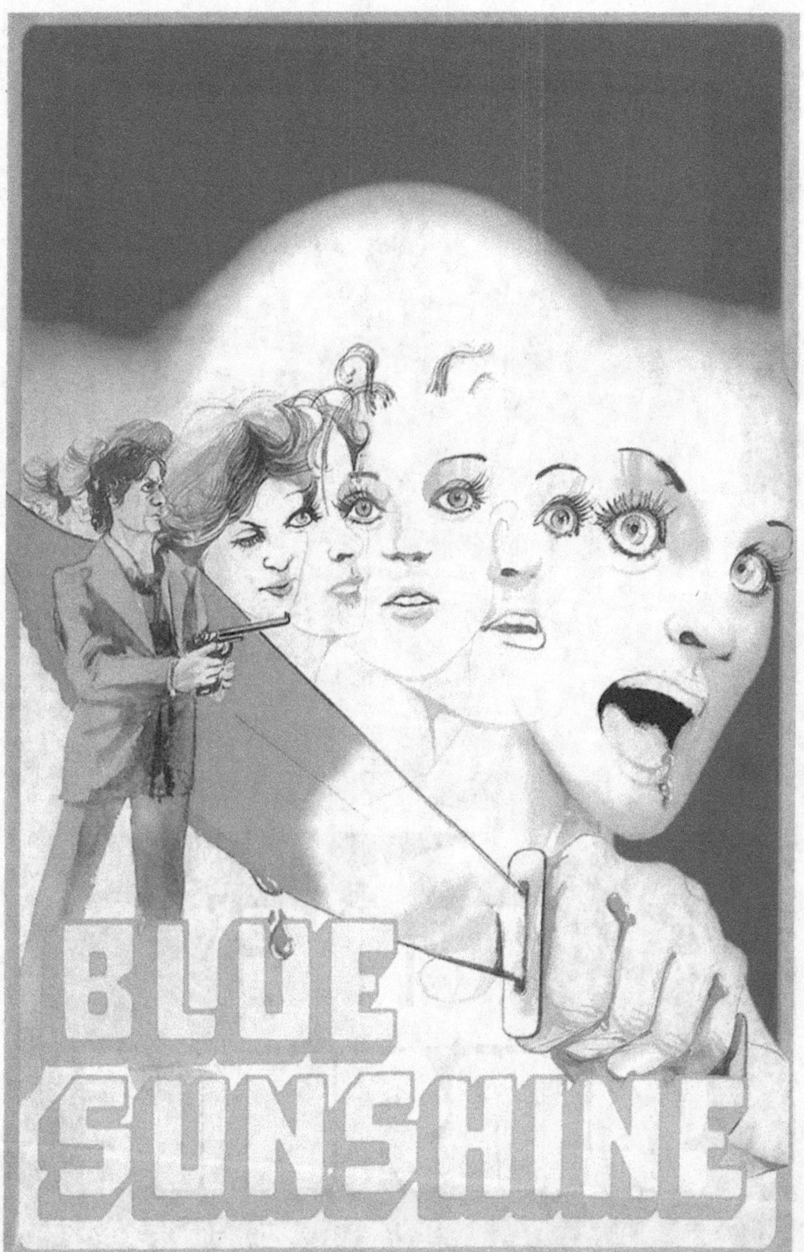

BLUE
SUNSHINE

BLUE SUNSHINE

blue sunshine x
A SHOCKER!
Ellanby Films presents
BLUE SUNSHINE, a film by Jeff Lieberman
starring Zalman King/Deborah Winters/
Mark Goddard/Robert Walden
Charles Siebert / Ann Cooper/Ray Young
Guest Stars Alice Ghostley and Stefan Gierasch.
Produced by George Manasse
Executive Producers Edgar Lansbury & Joseph Beruh

BLUE
SUNSHINE

ESCLUSIVITA VINCENT CINEMATOGRAFICA

SINDROME DEL TERRORE

CON ZALMAN KING · DEBORAH WINTERS · MARK GODDARD
ROBERT WALDEN · CHARLES SIEBERT · ANN COOPER
RAY YOUNG E CON ALICE GHOSTLEY · STEFAN GIERASCH
UN FILM DI JEFF LIEBERMAN   PRODOTTO DA GEORGE MANASSE
COLORE LA MICROSTAMPA

ZALMAN KING * DEBORAH WINTERS * MARK GODDARD
BLUE SUNSHINE

9 781960 721433